DISNEY MOANA

THE STORY OF THE MOVIE IN COMICS

DARK HORSE BOOKS

To its inhabitants, Motunui is more than just an island—it's their whole world; a paradise that gives them everything they need. Meet the ones who call Motunui home...

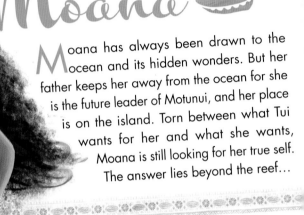

Moana

Moana has always been drawn to the ocean and its hidden wonders. But her father keeps her away from the ocean for she is the future leader of Motunui, and her place is on the island. Torn between what Tui wants for her and what she wants, Moana is still looking for her true self. The answer lies beyond the reef...

Tala

Tala is Moana's wise and unconventional grandmother who shares her special connection to the ocean. Tala knows well the heritage of her people, while most of the islanders have chosen to forget it. Her stories feed Moana's imagination and will help her make the right decision when the time comes.

Chief Tui and Sina

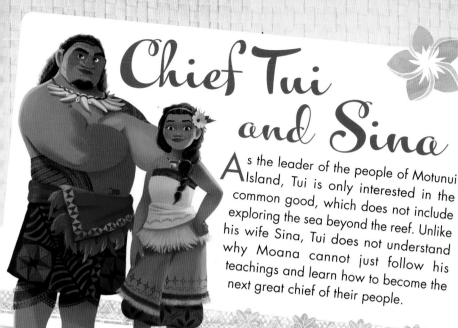

As the leader of the people of Motunui Island, Tui is only interested in the common good, which does not include exploring the sea beyond the reef. Unlike his wife Sina, Tui does not understand why Moana cannot just follow his teachings and learn how to become the next great chief of their people.

Pua

This small, adorable pig is Moana's loyal pet & friend. Not afraid of water or boats, Pua is always ready to jump on a canoe to help Moana achieve her heart's desire: to reach the open ocean!

Heihei

Heihei is not like any other chicken. He's dumber. If there's one way to get into danger, Heihei will find it. If there are two, he will find both of them. And still, there's no logical reason behind his actions. Yet, Moana believes there's more to him than meets the eye and that he does not deserve to be cooked and eaten!

The world beyond the reef is dangerous and unforgiving, home to horrible monsters and those far more powerful than humans...

Maui

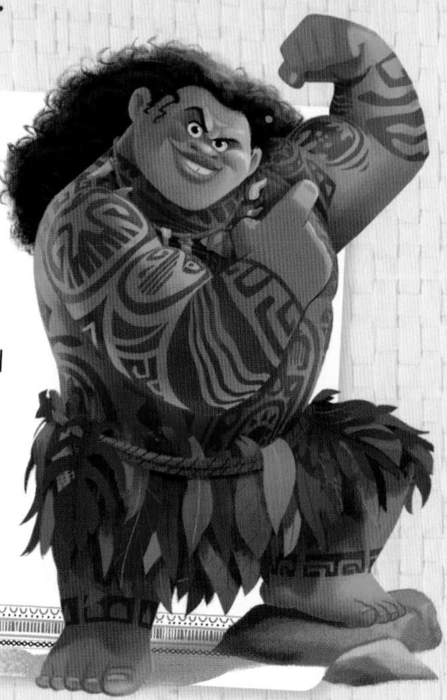

Once the greatest hero in Oceania, Maui is now just a legend, a forgotten demigod. After stealing the heart of Te Fiti, Maui has been confined to a small island, his only friend being one of his tattoos, a mini version of himself. Maui just wants to forget about his past and recover his magical fishhook, which allows him to shape-shift into all kinds of animals.

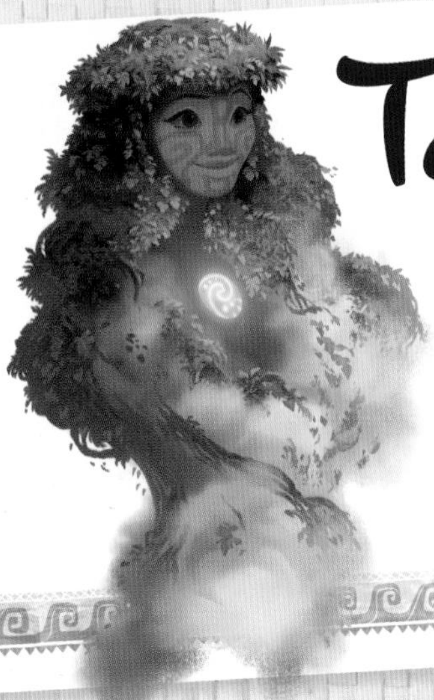

Te Fiti

Te Fiti, the mother island, emerged from the ocean at the beginning of time and created life. She made plants, humans, and animals flourish. But when Maui stole her heart, darkness began to spread among the islands...

Kakamora

They may look cute when you look at them from a distance, but these little warriors are just murdering pirates! They paint angry faces on their coconut-shell armor and attack any vessel crossing their waters to the dreadful beat of their big drums.

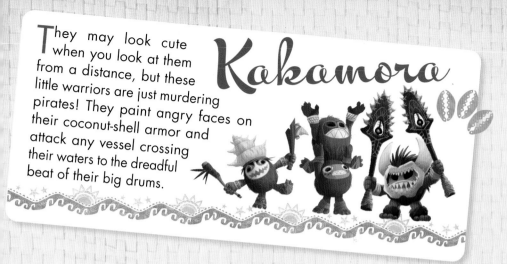

Tamatoa

Tamatoa is a scavenger, a collector of treasures, who lives in Lalotai, the land of monsters. He is obsessed with any shiny object that can make him as sparkly as a diamond. When Maui lost his precious hook, Tamatoa found it and added it to his collection.

Te kā

Te Kā is a gigantic lava monster, a demon of earth and fire. Surrounded by ash clouds and volcanic lightning, Te Kā walks on land and cannot touch water. A very long time ago, Te Kā defeated Maui, separating him from his hook.

"I am Moana of Motunui, you will board my boat... sail across the sea and restore the heart of Te Fiti."

-Moana

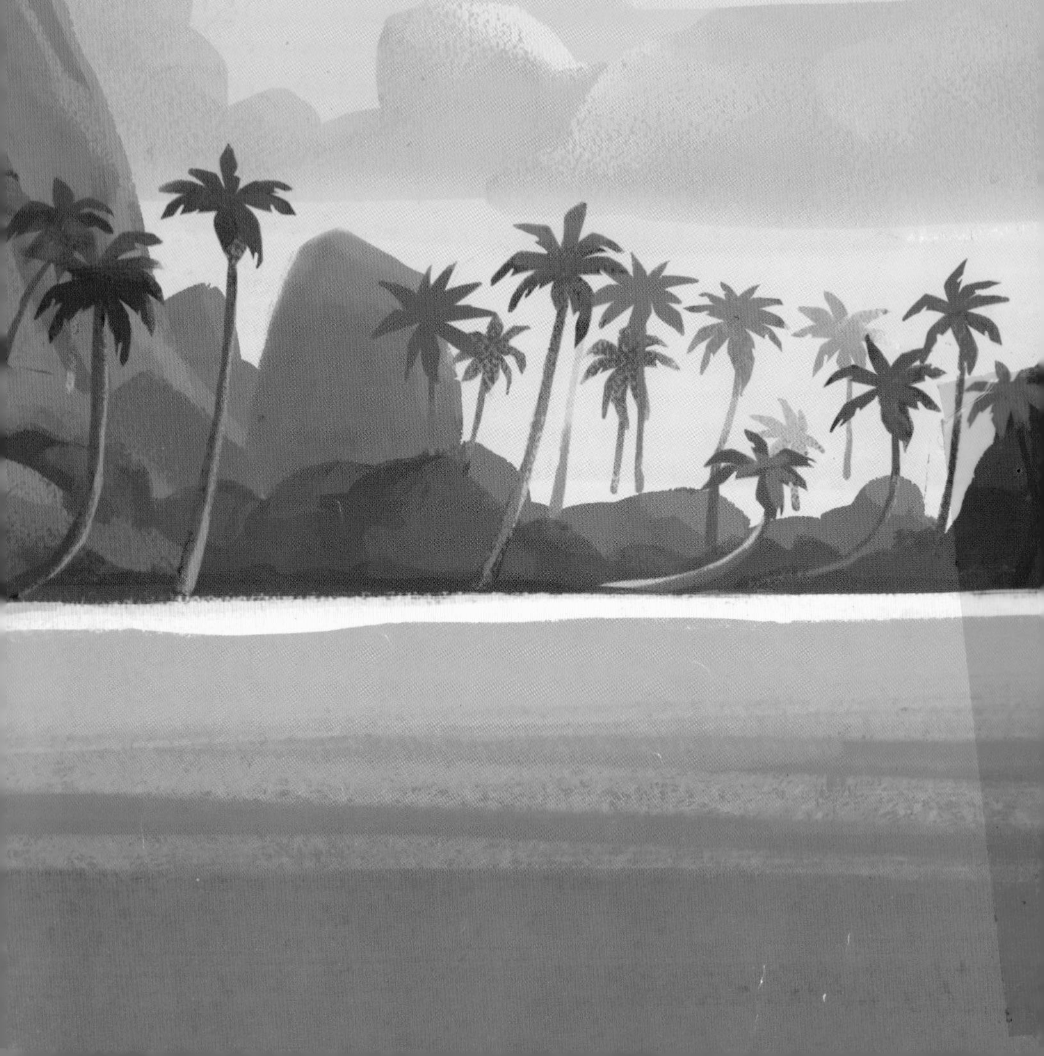

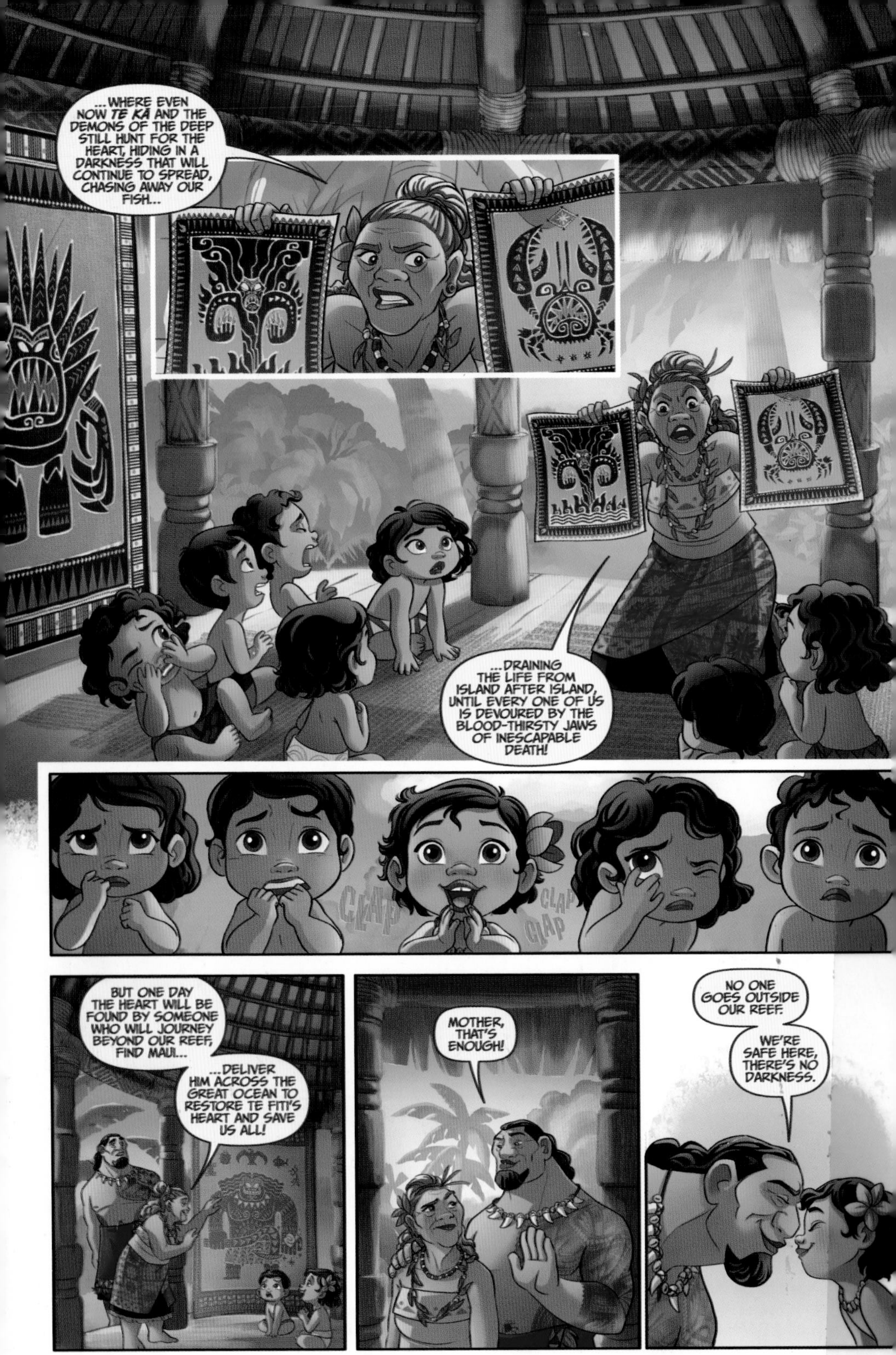
...WHERE EVEN NOW TE KĀ AND THE DEMONS OF THE DEEP STILL HUNT FOR THE HEART, HIDING IN A DARKNESS THAT WILL CONTINUE TO SPREAD, CHASING AWAY OUR FISH...
...DRAINING THE LIFE FROM ISLAND AFTER ISLAND, UNTIL EVERY ONE OF US IS DEVOURED BY THE BLOOD-THIRSTY JAWS OF INESCAPABLE DEATH!
CLAP
CLAP
CLAP
BUT ONE DAY THE HEART WILL BE FOUND BY SOMEONE WHO WILL JOURNEY BEYOND OUR REEF, FIND MAUI...
...DELIVER HIM ACROSS THE GREAT OCEAN TO RESTORE TE FITI'S HEART AND SAVE US ALL!
MOTHER, THAT'S ENOUGH!
NO ONE GOES OUTSIDE OUR REEF.
WE'RE SAFE HERE, THERE'S NO DARKNESS.

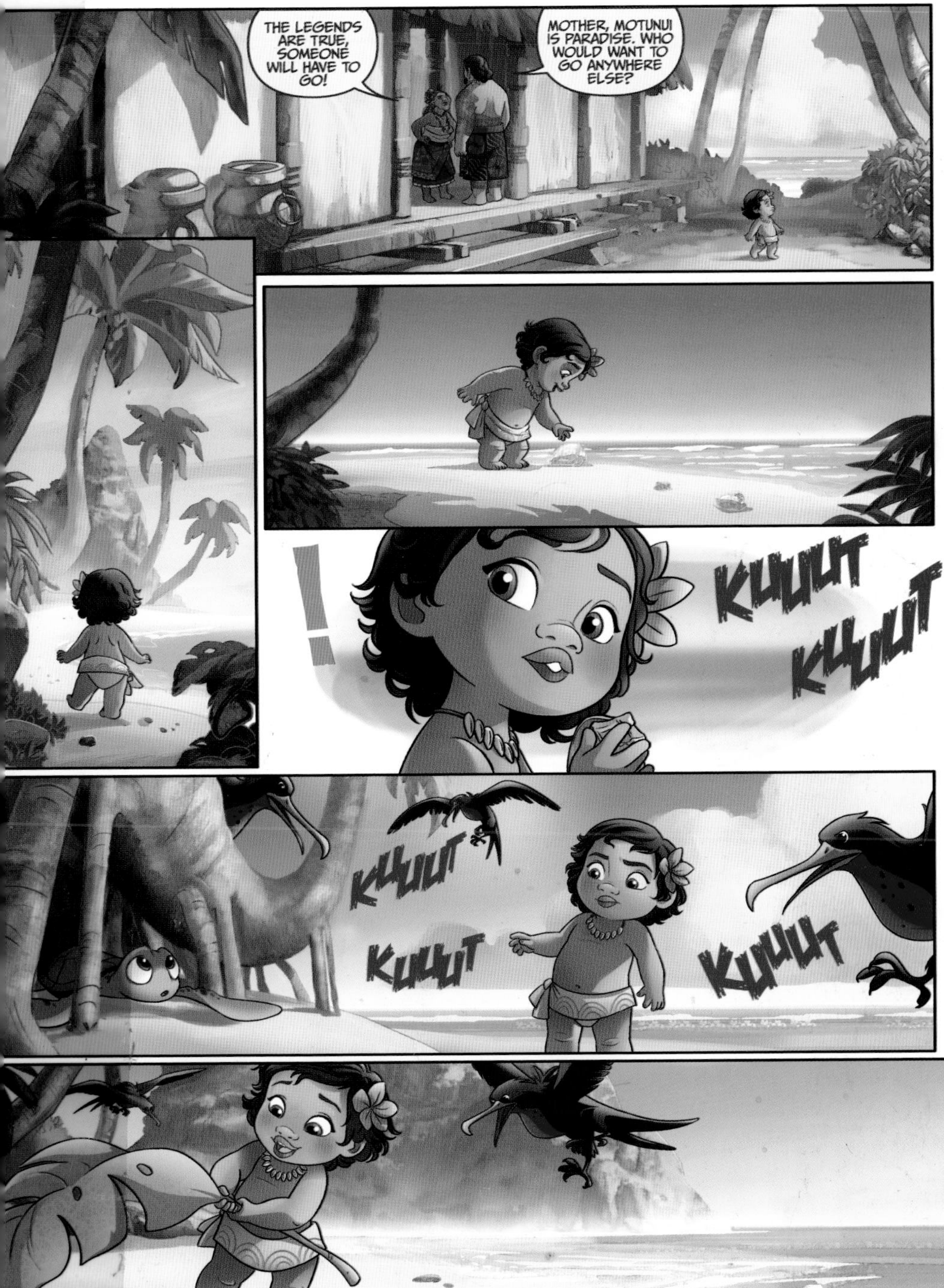
THE LEGENDS ARE TRUE, SOMEONE WILL HAVE TO GO!
MOTHER, MOTUNUI IS PARADISE. WHO WOULD WANT TO GO ANYWHERE ELSE?
!
KUUUT
KUUUT
KUUUT
KUUUT
KUUUT

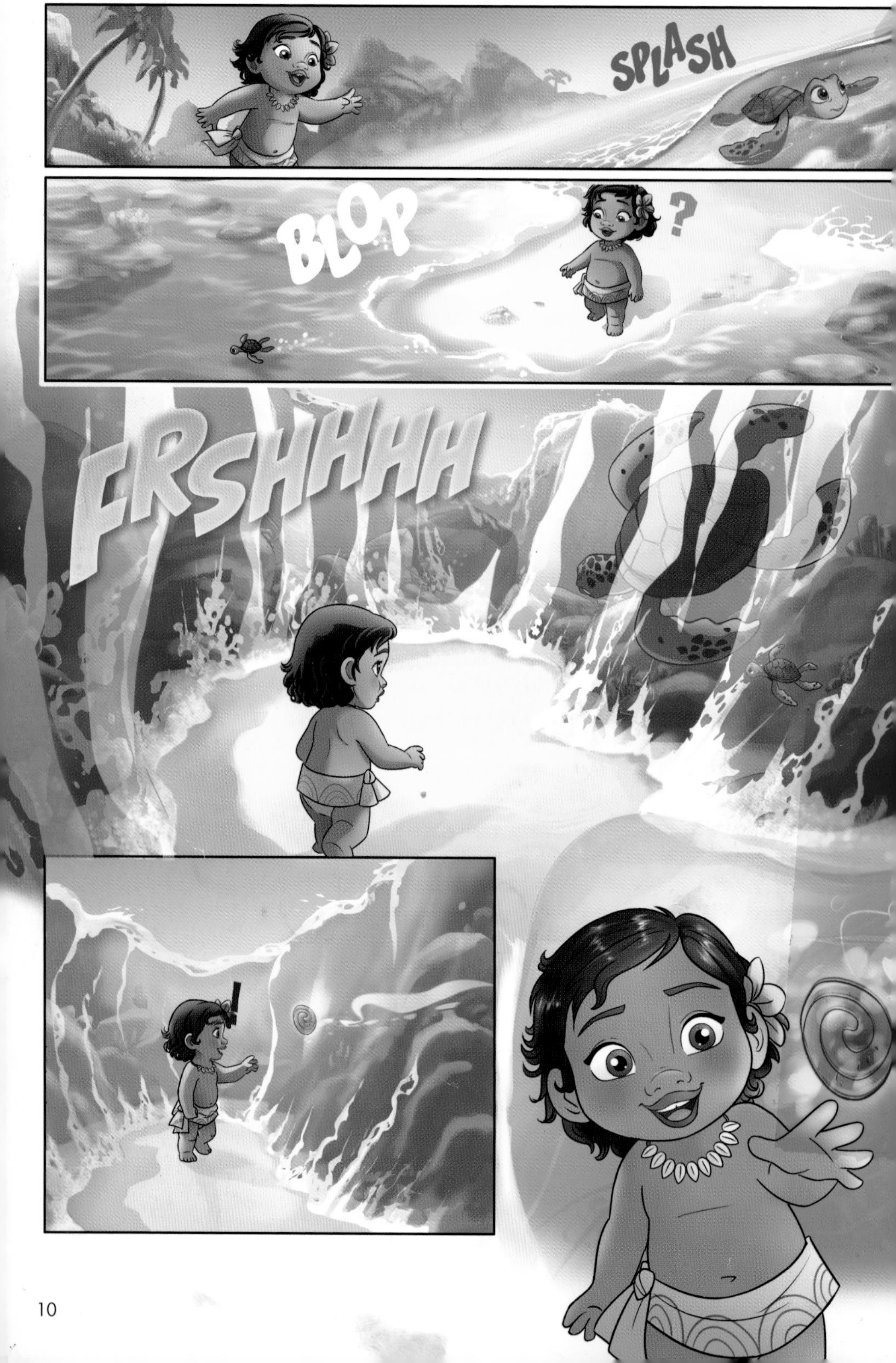
SPLASH
BLOP
?
FRSHHHH
!

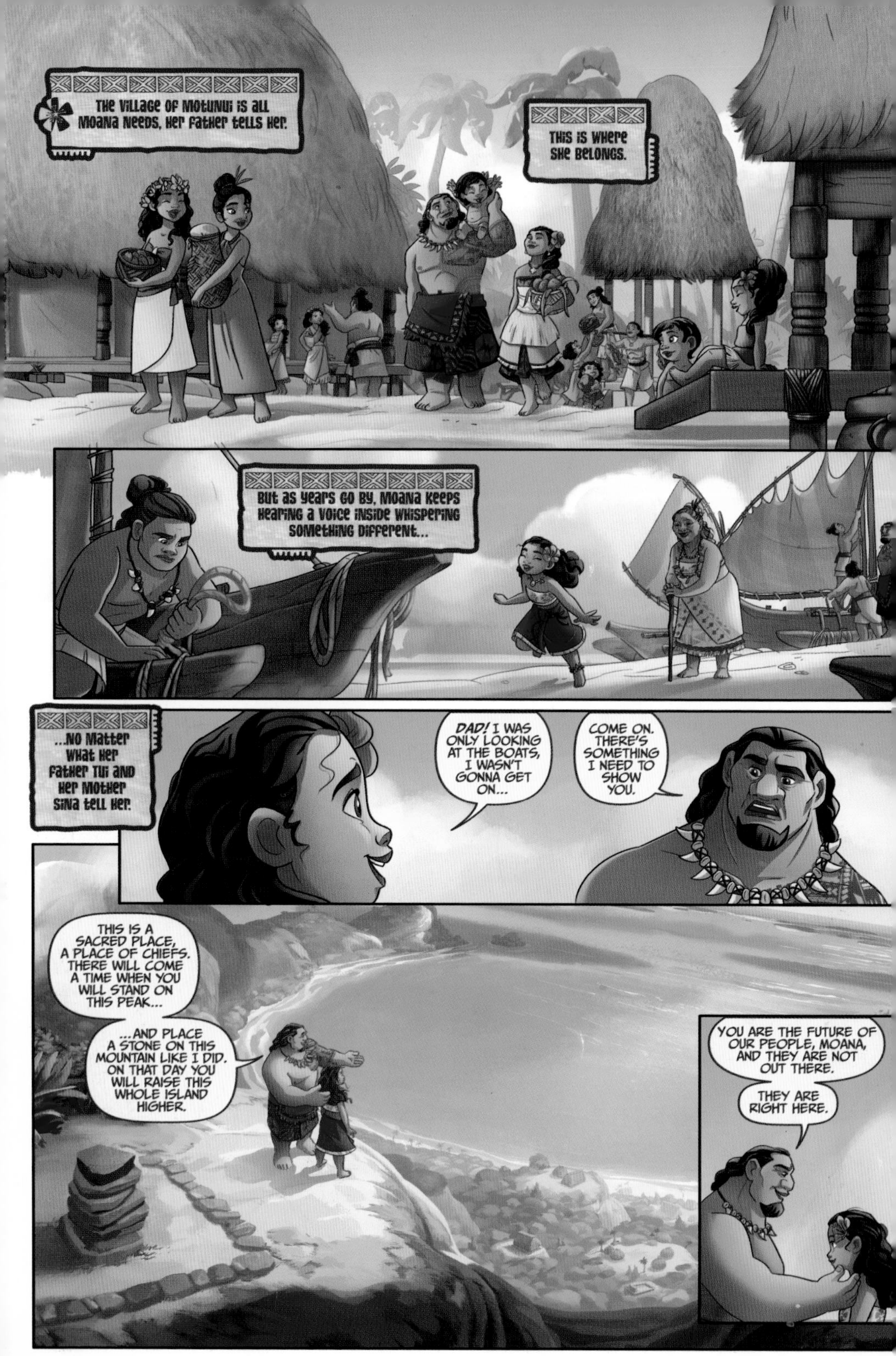

The Village of Motunui is all Moana needs, her father tells her.
This is where she belongs.
But as years go by, Moana keeps hearing a voice inside whispering something different...
...no matter what her father Tui and her mother Sina tell her.
DAD! I WAS ONLY LOOKING AT THE BOATS, I WASN'T GONNA GET ON...
COME ON. THERE'S SOMETHING I NEED TO SHOW YOU.
THIS IS A SACRED PLACE, A PLACE OF CHIEFS. THERE WILL COME A TIME WHEN YOU WILL STAND ON THIS PEAK...
...AND PLACE A STONE ON THIS MOUNTAIN LIKE I DID. ON THAT DAY YOU WILL RAISE THIS WHOLE ISLAND HIGHER.
YOU ARE THE FUTURE OF OUR PEOPLE, MOANA, AND THEY ARE NOT OUT THERE.
THEY ARE RIGHT HERE.

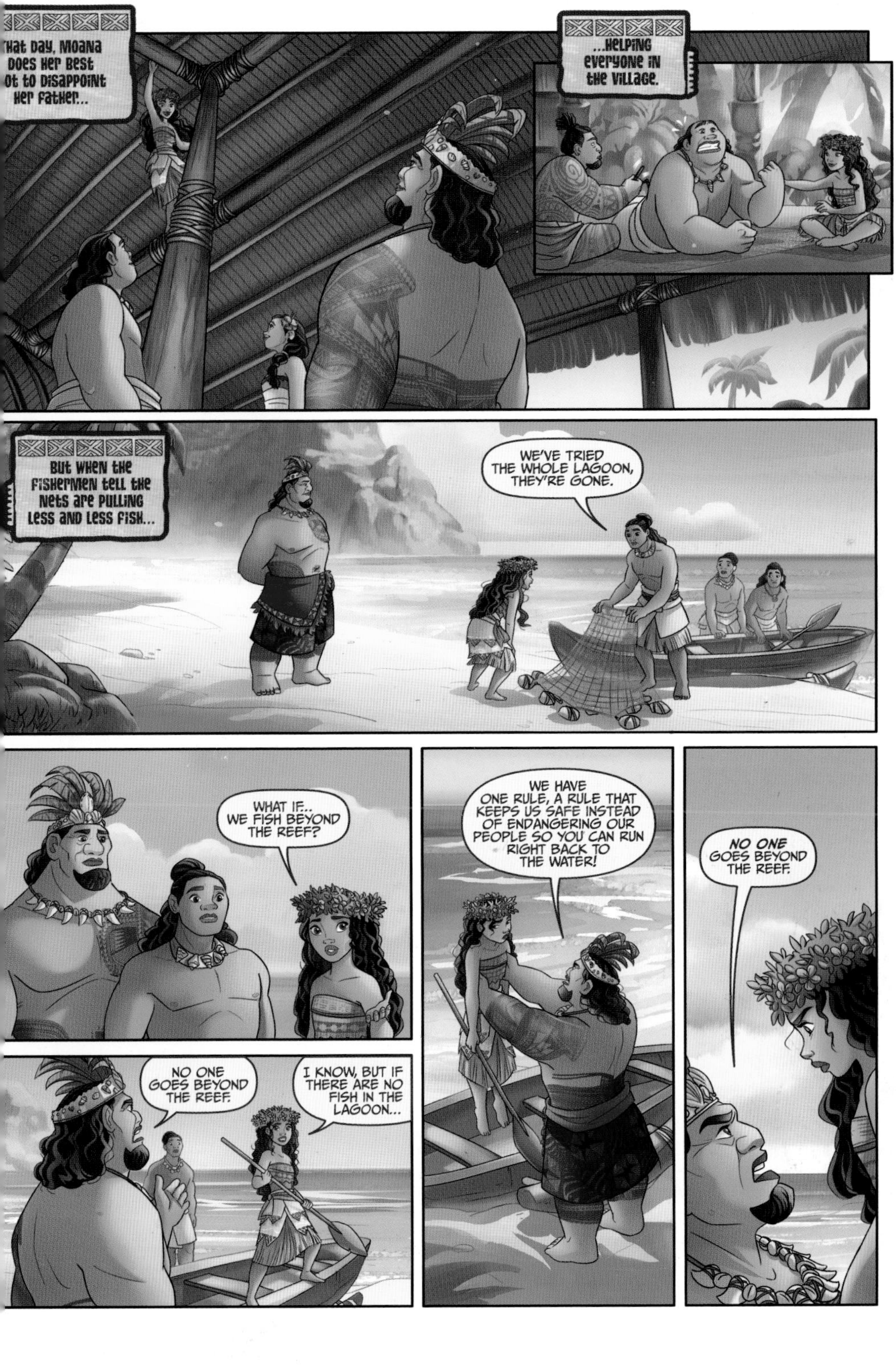
That day, Moana does her best ot to disappoint her father...
...helping everyone in the village.
But when the fishermen tell the nets are pulling less and less fish...
WE'VE TRIED THE WHOLE LAGOON, THEY'RE GONE.
WHAT IF... WE FISH BEYOND THE REEF?
NO ONE GOES BEYOND THE REEF.
I KNOW, BUT IF THERE ARE NO FISH IN THE LAGOON...
WE HAVE ONE RULE, A RULE THAT KEEPS US SAFE INSTEAD OF ENDANGERING OUR PEOPLE SO YOU CAN RUN RIGHT BACK TO THE WATER!
NO ONE GOES BEYOND THE REEF.

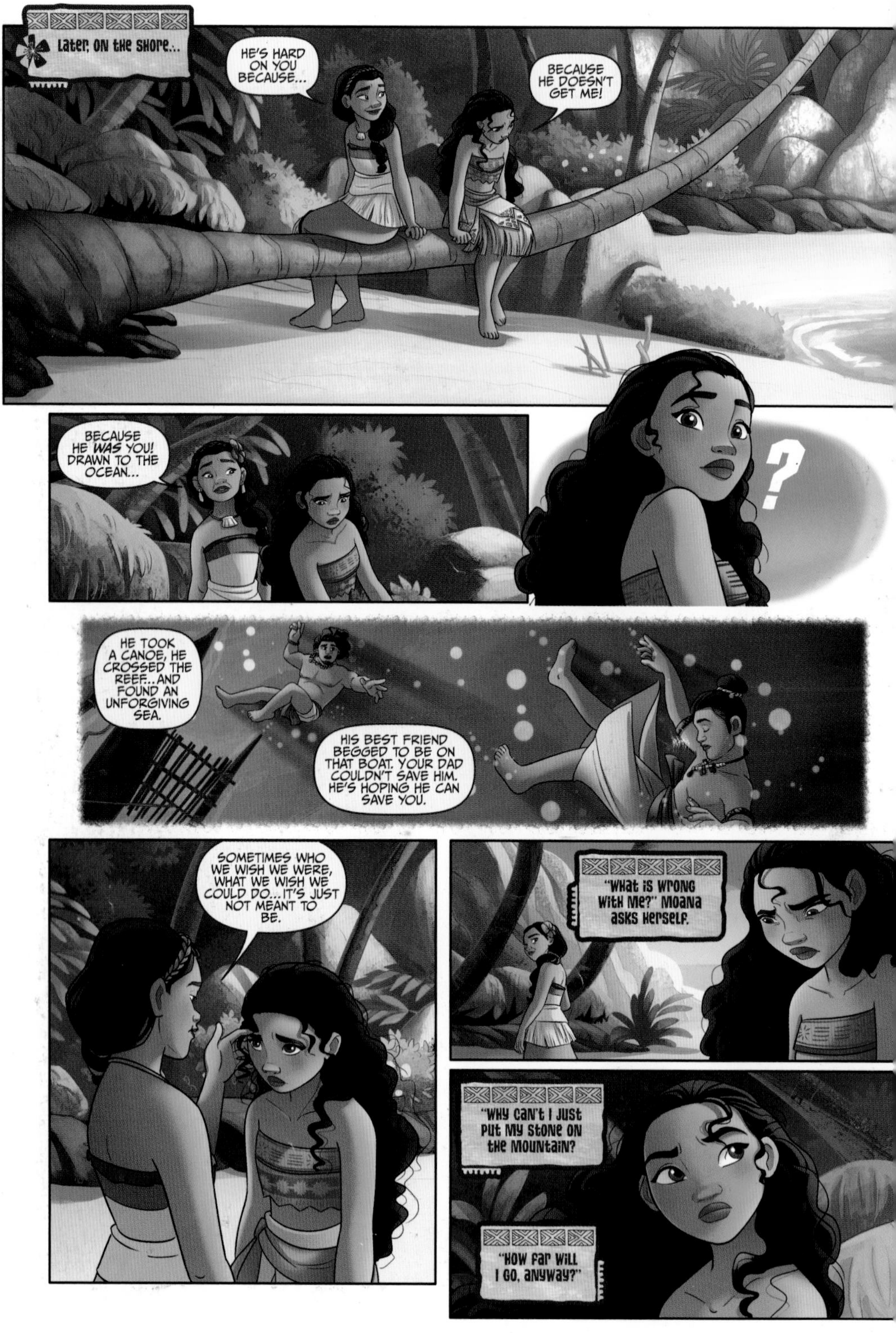
Later, on the shore...
HE'S HARD ON YOU BECAUSE...
BECAUSE HE DOESN'T GET ME!
BECAUSE HE WAS YOU! DRAWN TO THE OCEAN...
?
HE TOOK A CANOE, HE CROSSED THE REEF...AND FOUND AN UNFORGIVING SEA.
HIS BEST FRIEND BEGGED TO BE ON THAT BOAT. YOUR DAD COULDN'T SAVE HIM. HE'S HOPING HE CAN SAVE YOU.
SOMETIMES WHO WE WISH WE WERE, WHAT WE WISH WE COULD DO... IT'S JUST NOT MEANT TO BE.
"What is wrong with me?" Moana asks herself.
"Why can't I just put my stone on the mountain?
"How far will I go, anyway?"

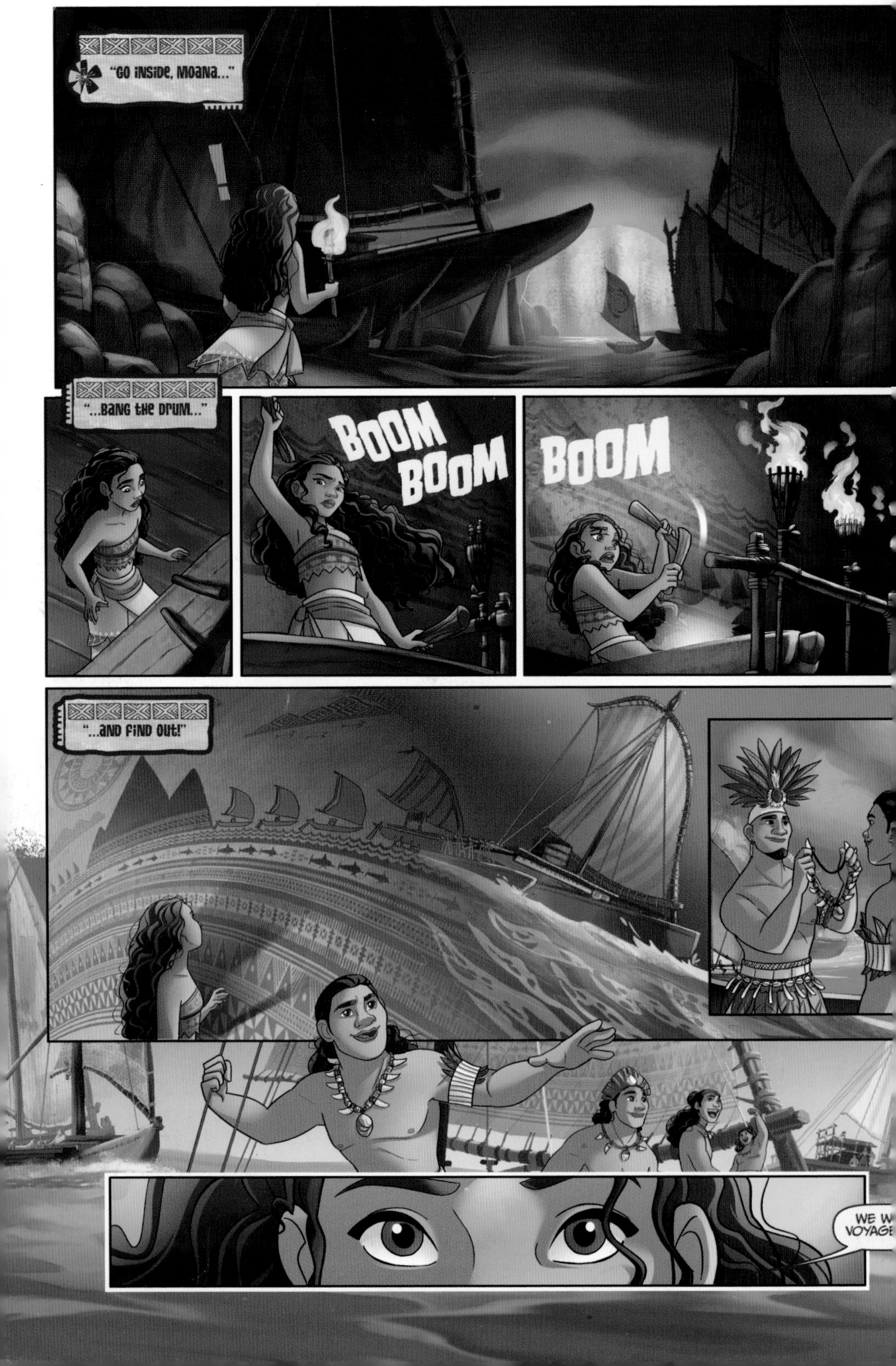
"GO INSIDE, MOANA..."
"...BANG THE DRUM..."
BOOM
BOOM
BOOM
"...AND FIND OUT!"

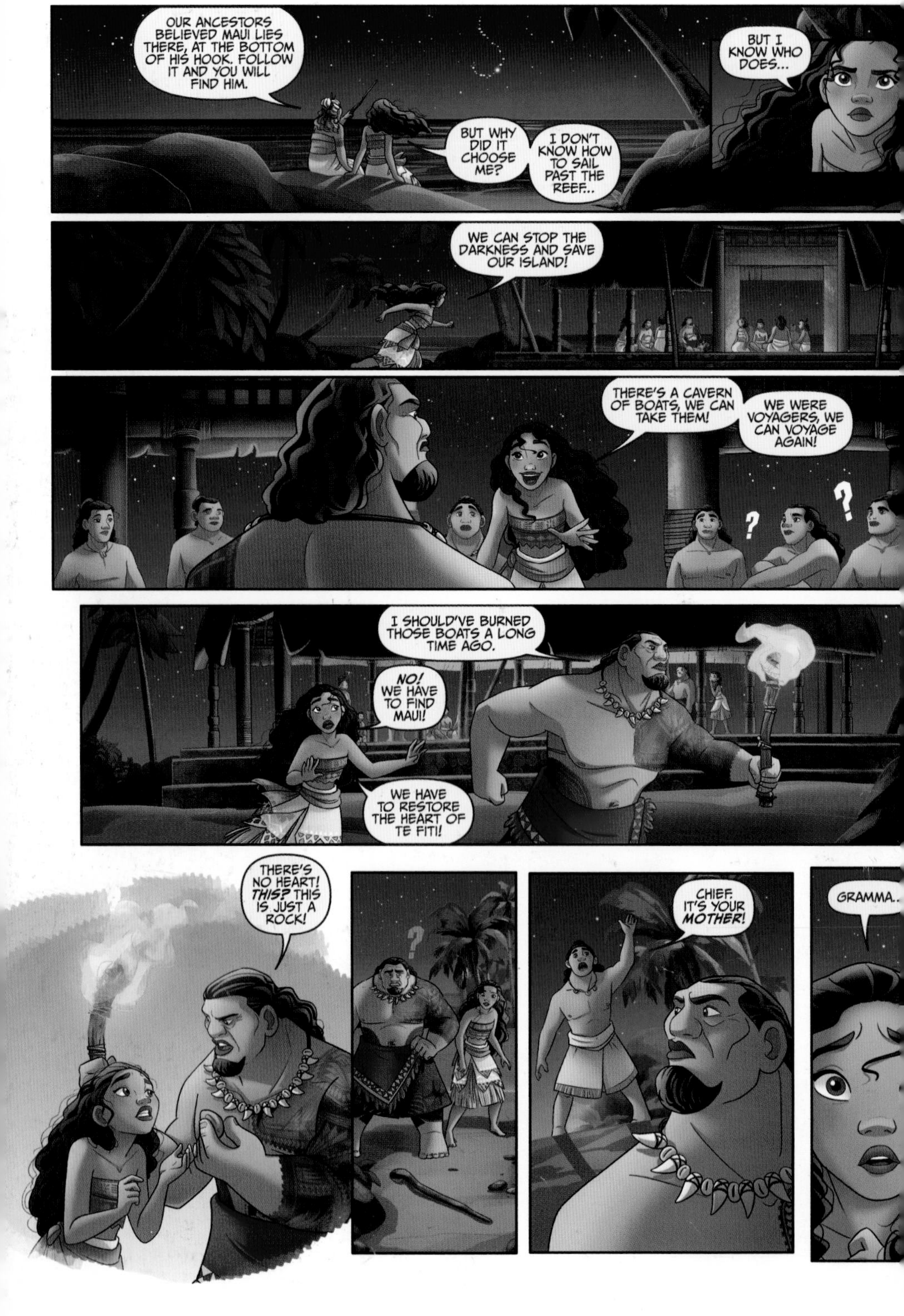
OUR ANCESTORS BELIEVED MAUI LIES THERE, AT THE BOTTOM OF HIS HOOK. FOLLOW IT AND YOU WILL FIND HIM.
BUT WHY DID IT CHOOSE ME?
I DON'T KNOW HOW TO SAIL PAST THE REEF...
BUT I KNOW WHO DOES...
WE CAN STOP THE DARKNESS AND SAVE OUR ISLAND!
THERE'S A CAVERN OF BOATS, WE CAN TAKE THEM!
WE WERE VOYAGERS, WE CAN VOYAGE AGAIN!
?
?
I SHOULD'VE BURNED THOSE BOATS A LONG TIME AGO.
NO! WE HAVE TO FIND MAUI!
WE HAVE TO RESTORE THE HEART OF TE FITI!
THERE'S NO HEART! THIS? THIS IS JUST A ROCK!
?
CHIEF. IT'S YOUR MOTHER!
GRAMMA...

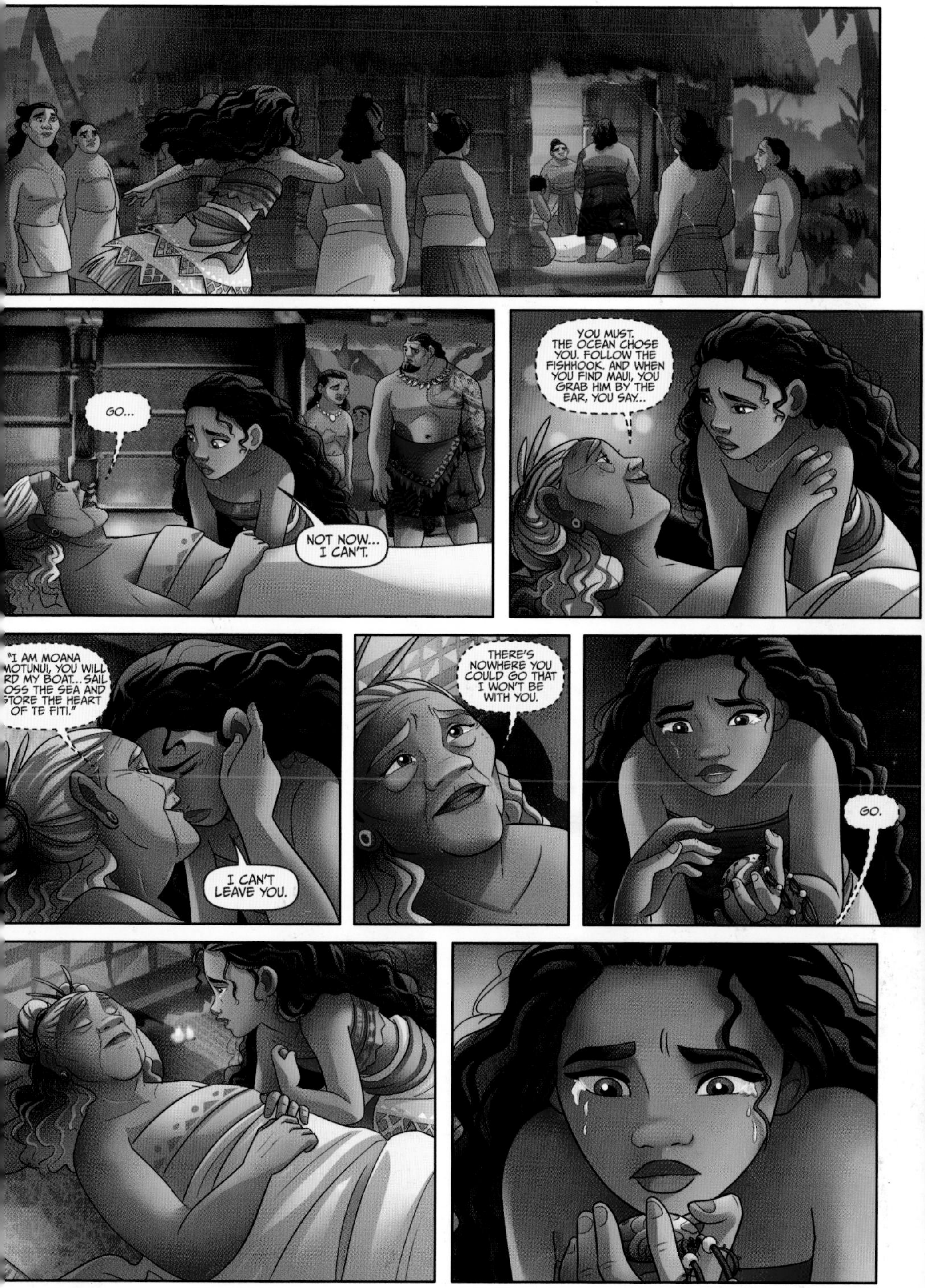
GO...
NOT NOW... I CAN'T.
YOU MUST. THE OCEAN CHOSE YOU. FOLLOW THE FISHHOOK. AND WHEN YOU FIND MAUI, YOU GRAB HIM BY THE EAR, YOU SAY...
"I AM MOANA MOTUNUI, YOU WILL RD MY BOAT... SAIL OSS THE SEA AND STORE THE HEART OF TE FITI."
I CAN'T LEAVE YOU.
THERE'S NOWHERE YOU COULD GO THAT I WON'T BE WITH YOU.
GO.

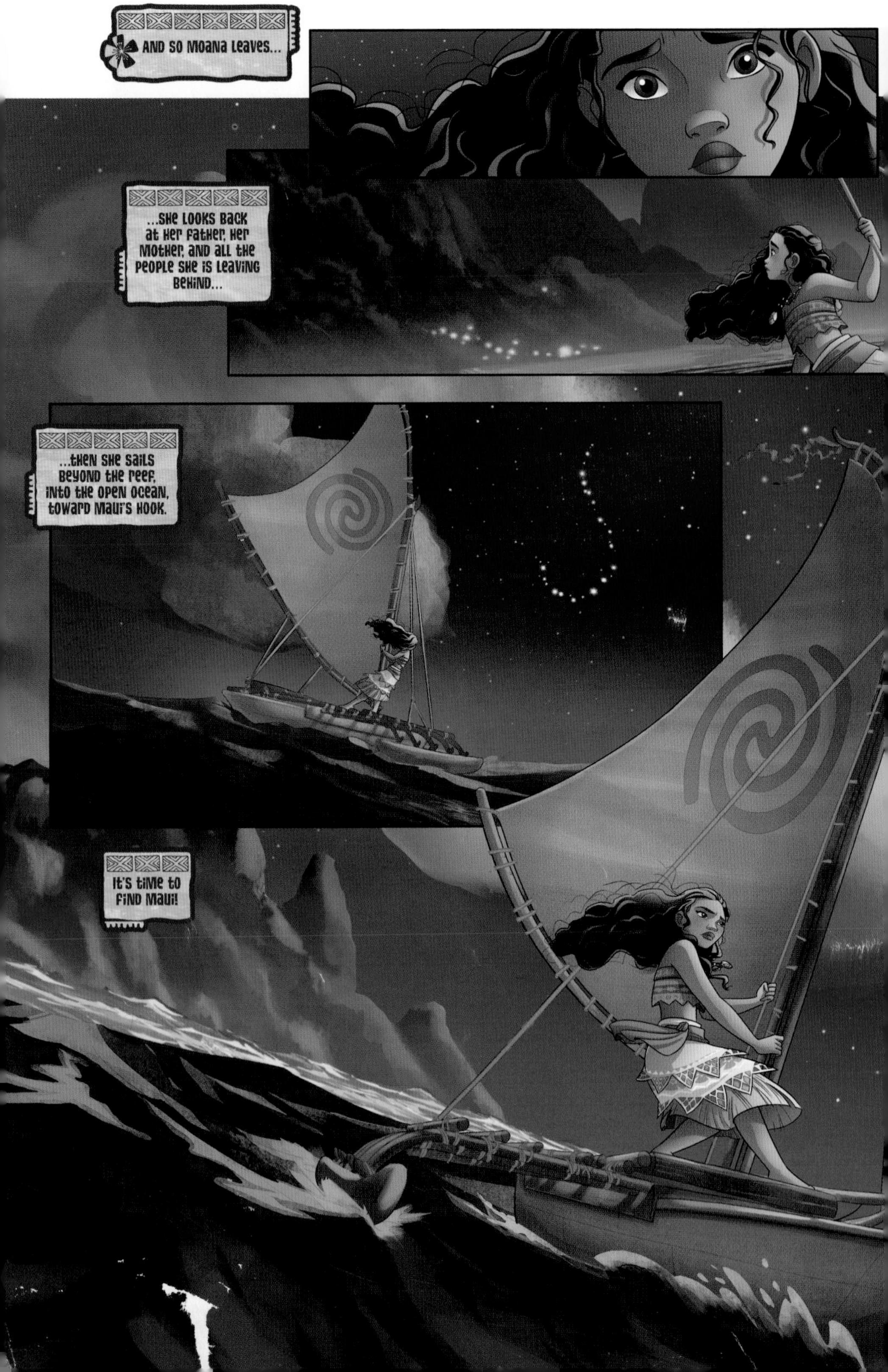
AND SO MOANA LEAVES...
...SHE LOOKS BACK AT HER FATHER, HER MOTHER, AND ALL THE PEOPLE SHE IS LEAVING BEHIND...
...THEN SHE SAILS BEYOND THE REEF, INTO THE OPEN OCEAN, TOWARD MAUI'S HOOK.
IT'S TIME TO FIND MAUI!

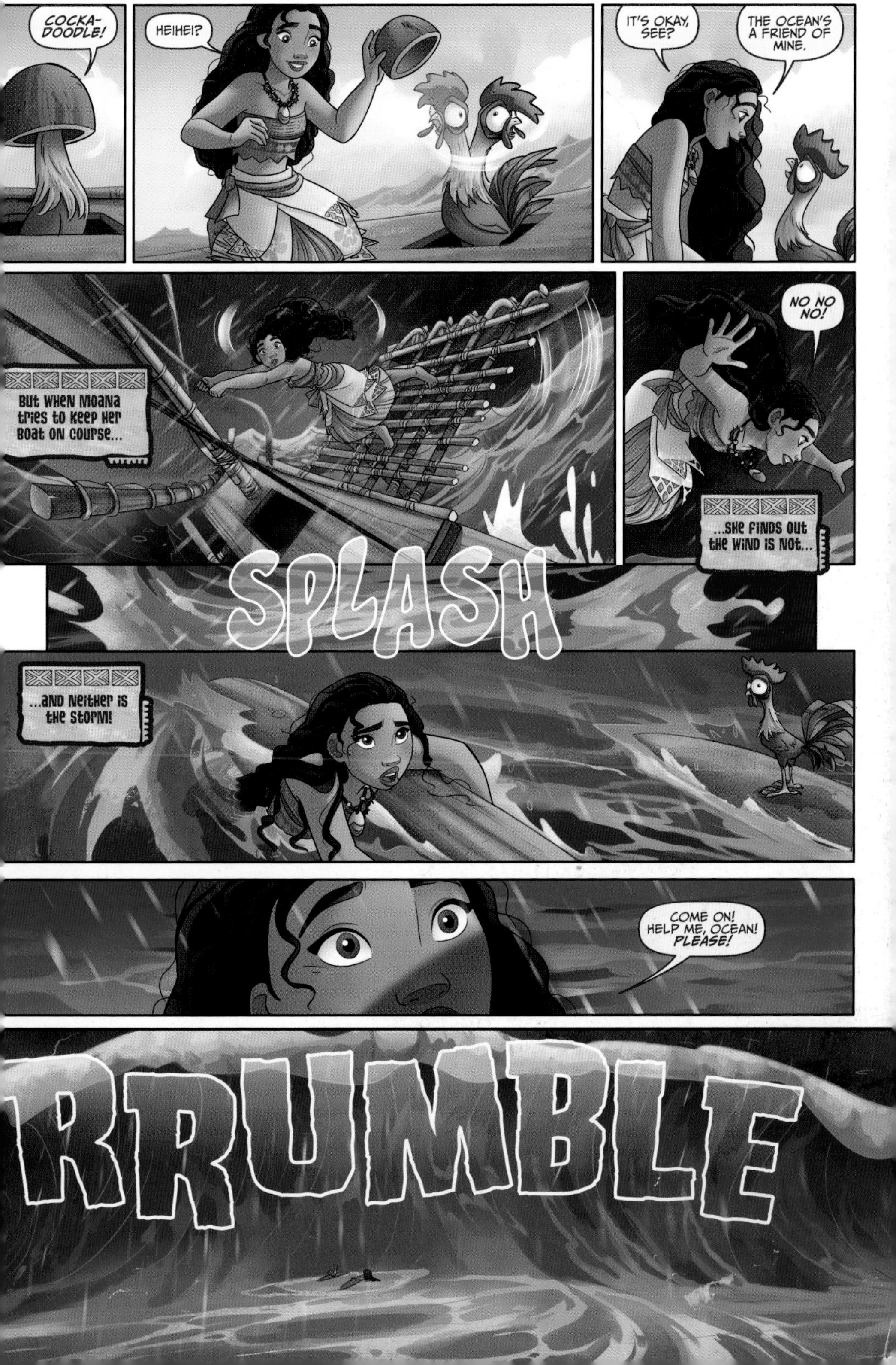
COCKA-DOODLE!
HEIHEI?
IT'S OKAY, SEE?
THE OCEAN'S A FRIEND OF MINE.
But when Moana tries to keep her boat on course...
NO NO NO!
...she finds out the wind is not...
SPLASH
...and neither is the storm!
COME ON! HELP ME, OCEAN! PLEASE!
RRUMBLE

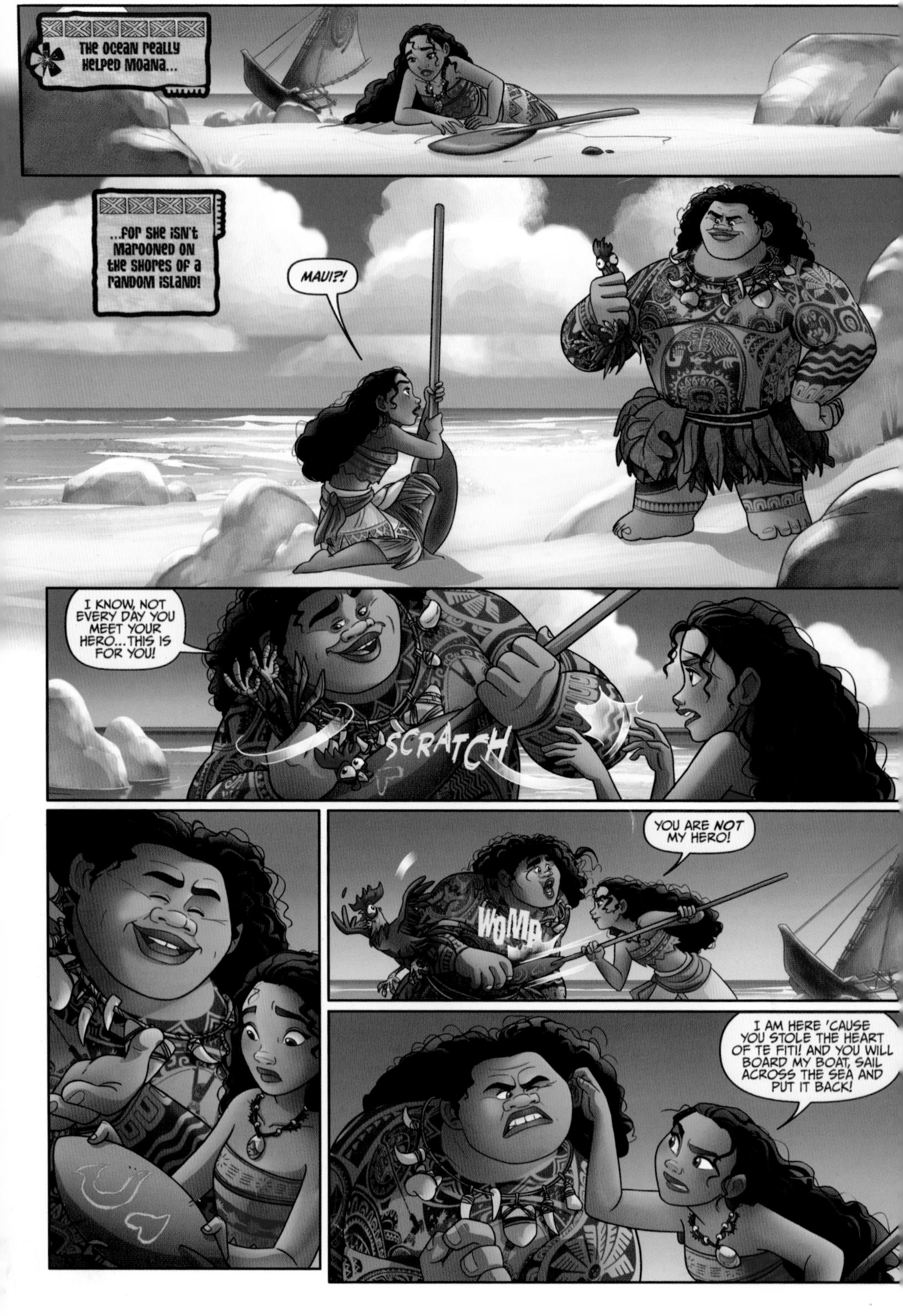

The Ocean really helped Moana...
...for she isn't marooned on the shores of a random island!
MAUI?!
I KNOW, NOT EVERY DAY YOU MEET YOUR HERO...THIS IS FOR YOU!
SCRATCH
YOU ARE NOT MY HERO!
WOMP
I AM HERE 'CAUSE YOU STOLE THE HEART OF TE FITI! AND YOU WILL BOARD MY BOAT, SAIL ACROSS THE SEA AND PUT IT BACK!

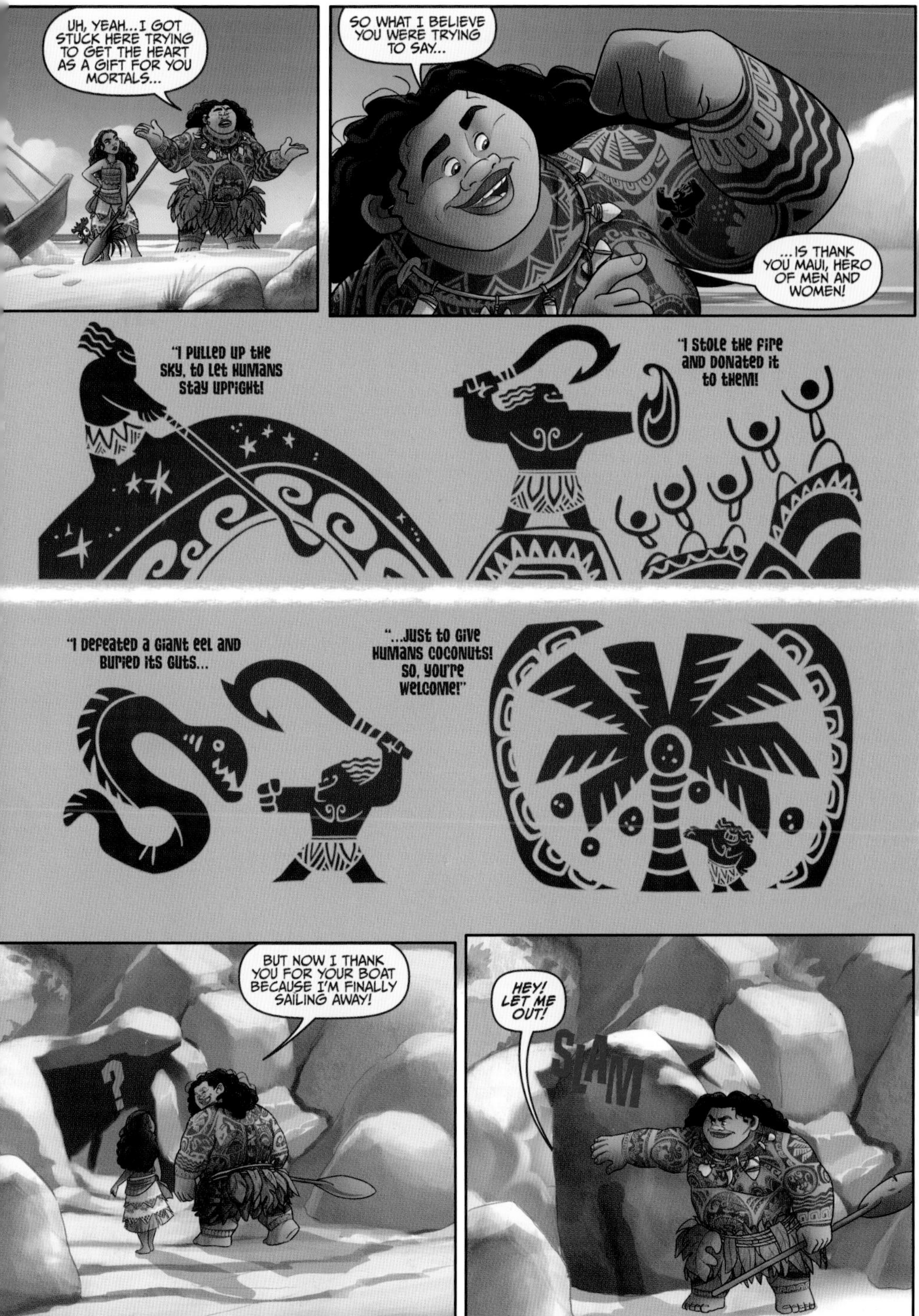
UH, YEAH...I GOT STUCK HERE TRYING TO GET THE HEART AS A GIFT FOR YOU MORTALS...
SO WHAT I BELIEVE YOU WERE TRYING TO SAY...
...IS THANK YOU MAUI, HERO OF MEN AND WOMEN!
"I PULLED UP THE SKY, TO LET HUMANS STAY UPRIGHT!
"I STOLE THE FIRE AND DONATED IT TO THEM!
"I DEFEATED A GIANT EEL AND BURIED ITS GUTS...
"...JUST TO GIVE HUMANS COCONUTS! SO, YOU'RE WELCOME!"
BUT NOW I THANK YOU FOR YOUR BOAT BECAUSE I'M FINALLY SAILING AWAY!
HEY! LET ME OUT!
SLAM

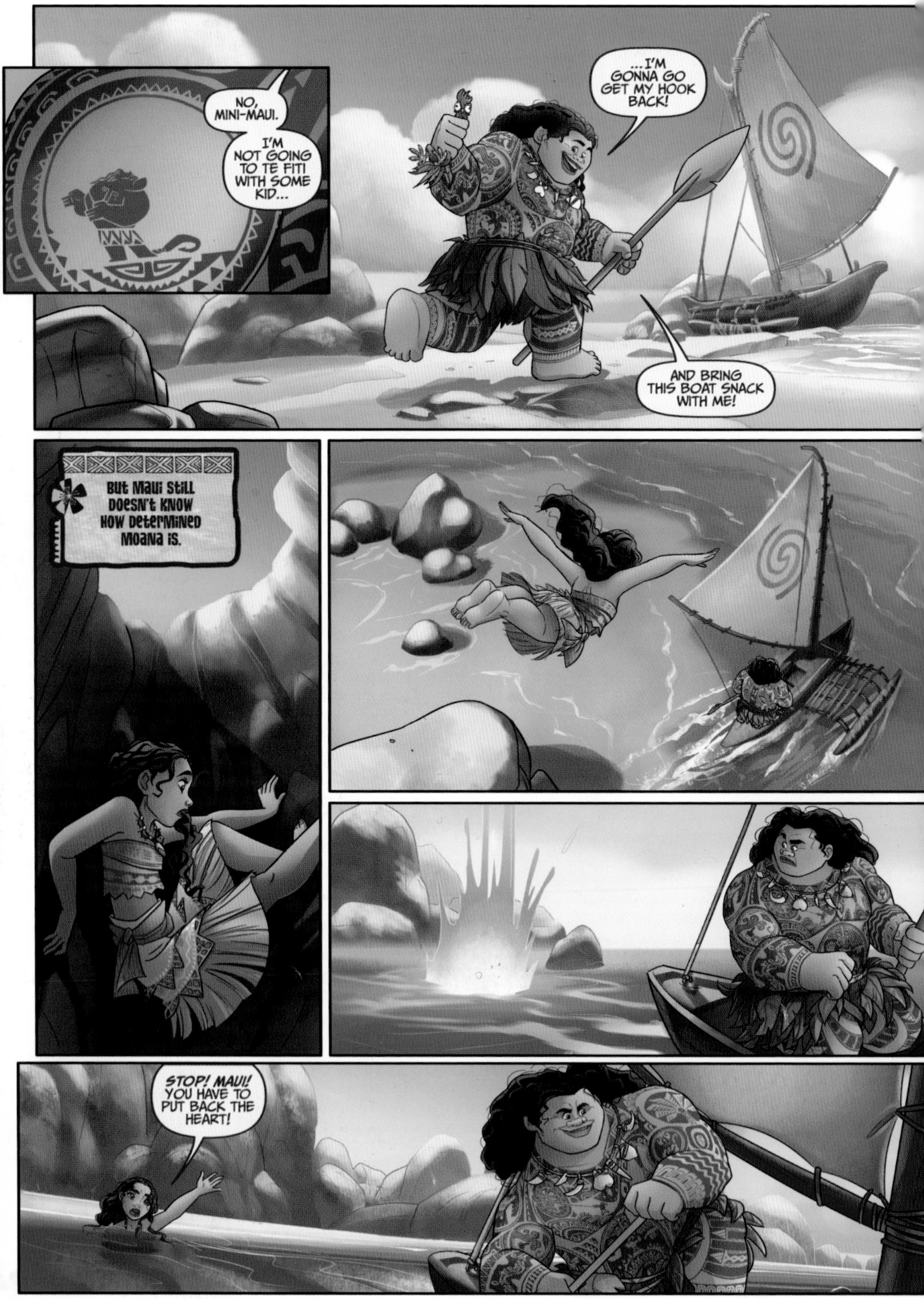

...I'M GONNA GO GET MY HOOK BACK!
NO, MINI-MAUI.
I'M NOT GOING TO TE FITI WITH SOME KID...
AND BRING THIS BOAT SNACK WITH ME!
But Maui still doesn't know how determined Moana is.
STOP! MAUI! YOU HAVE TO PUT BACK THE HEART!

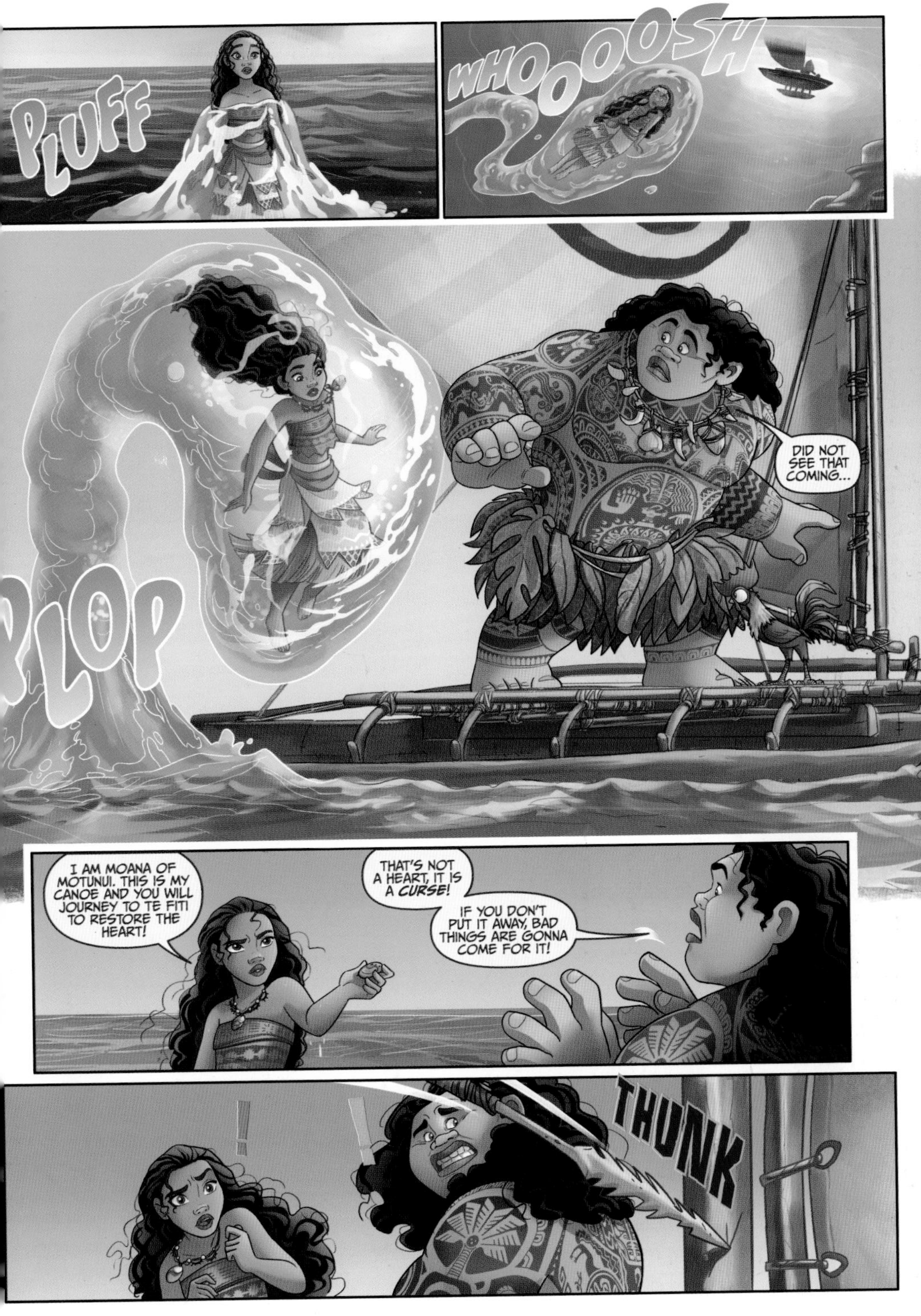
PLUFF
WHOOOOOSH
PLOP
DID NOT SEE THAT COMING...
I AM MOANA OF MOTUNUI. THIS IS MY CANOE AND YOU WILL JOURNEY TO TE FITI TO RESTORE THE HEART!
THAT'S NOT A HEART, IT IS A *CURSE*!
IF YOU DON'T PUT IT AWAY, BAD THINGS ARE GONNA COME FOR IT!
!
!
THUNK

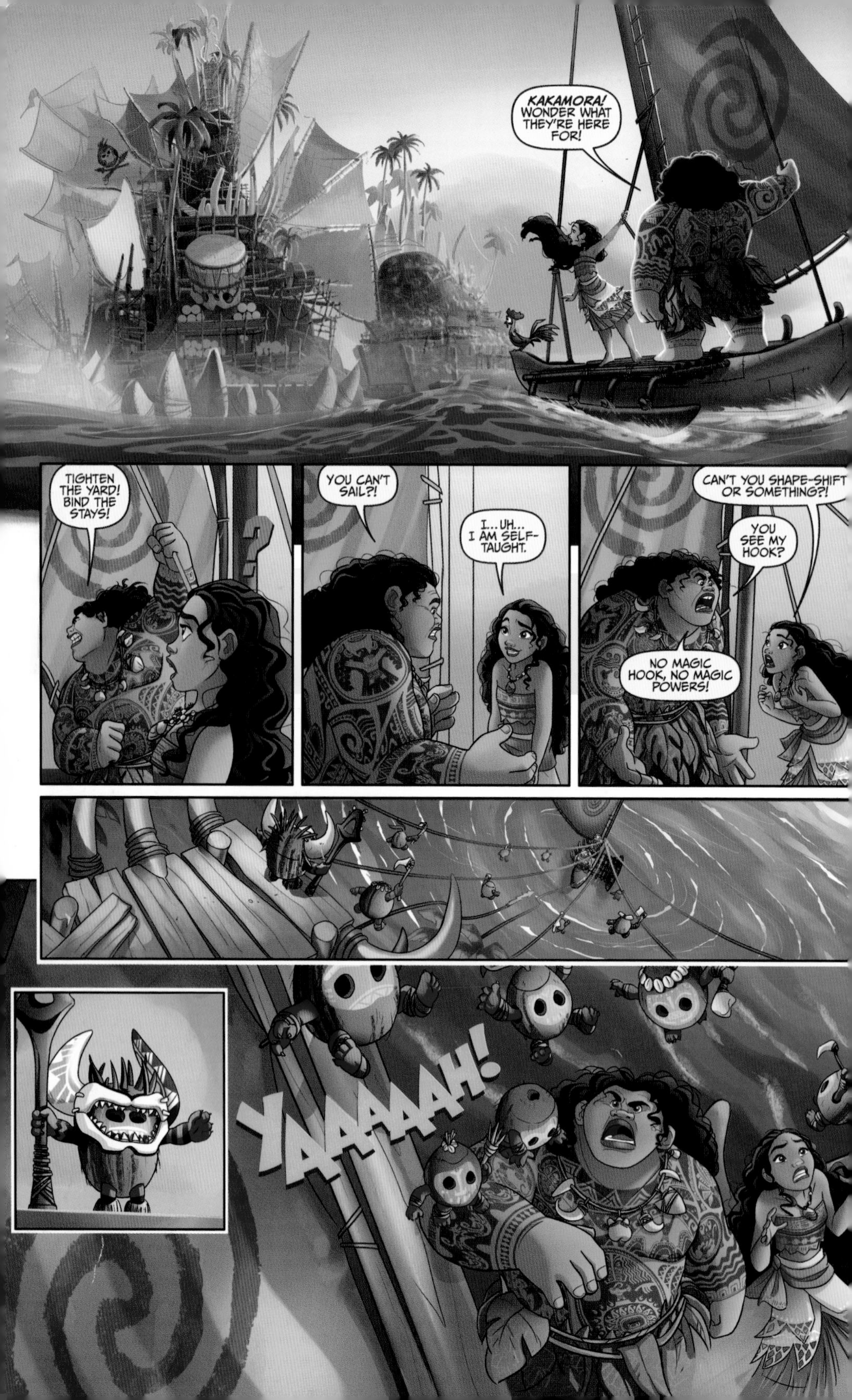
KAKAMORA! WONDER WHAT THEY'RE HERE FOR!
TIGHTEN THE YARD! BIND THE STAYS!
?
YOU CAN'T SAIL?!
I... UH... I AM SELF-TAUGHT.
CAN'T YOU SHAPE-SHIFT OR SOMETHING?!
YOU SEE MY HOOK?
NO MAGIC HOOK, NO MAGIC POWERS!
YAAAAAH!

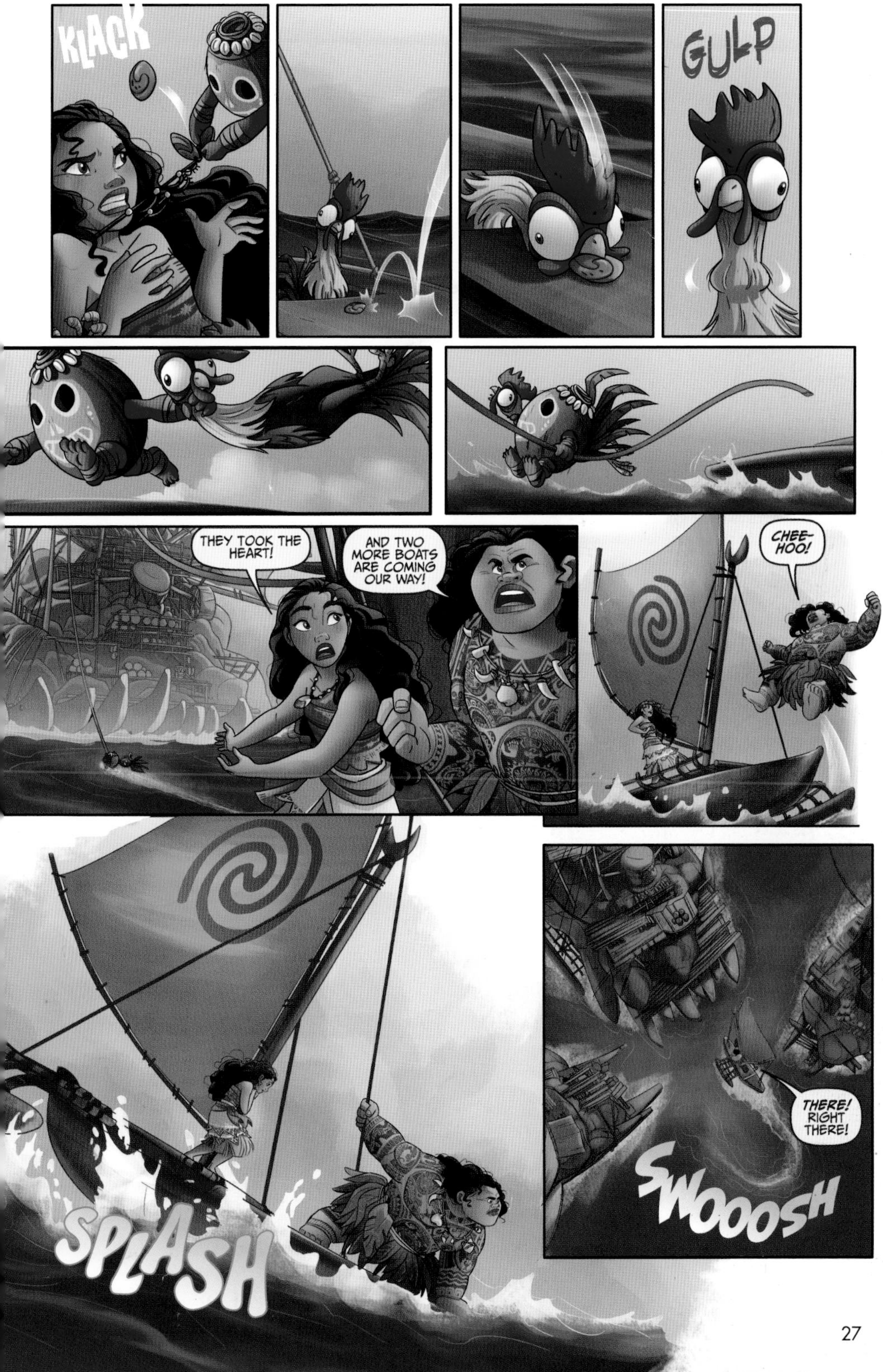
KLACK
GULP
THEY TOOK THE HEART!
AND TWO MORE BOATS ARE COMING OUR WAY!
CHEE-HOO!
SPLASH
THERE! RIGHT THERE!
SWOOOSH

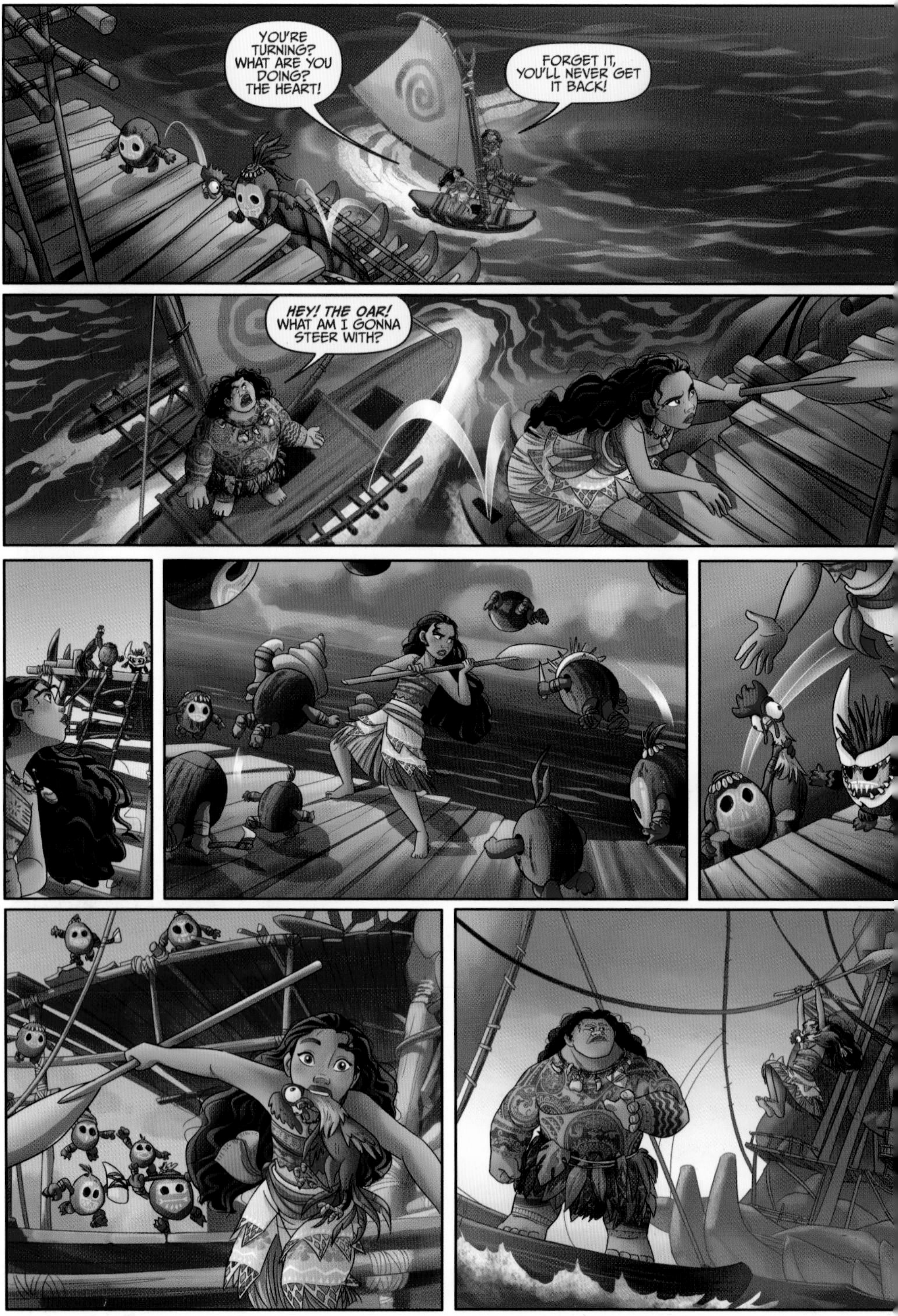
YOU'RE TURNING? WHAT ARE YOU DOING? THE HEART!
FORGET IT, YOU'LL NEVER GET IT BACK!
HEY! THE OAR! WHAT AM I GONNA STEER WITH?

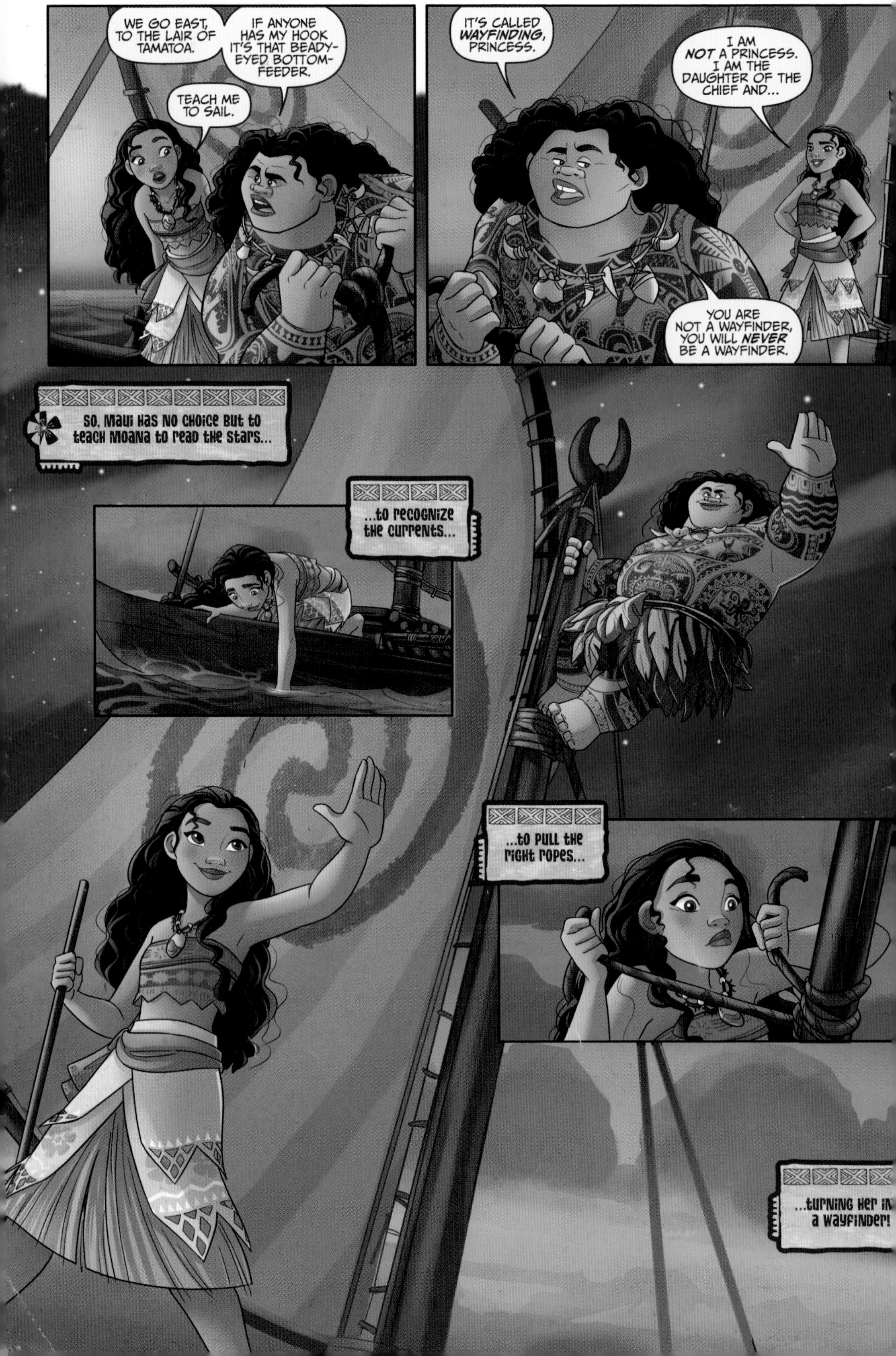
WE GO EAST, TO THE LAIR OF TAMATOA.
IF ANYONE HAS MY HOOK IT'S THAT BEADY-EYED BOTTOM-FEEDER.
TEACH ME TO SAIL.
IT'S CALLED *WAYFINDING*, PRINCESS.
I AM *NOT* A PRINCESS. I AM THE DAUGHTER OF THE CHIEF AND...
YOU ARE NOT A WAYFINDER, YOU WILL *NEVER* BE A WAYFINDER.
SO, MAUI HAS NO CHOICE BUT TO TEACH MOANA TO READ THE STARS...
...TO RECOGNIZE THE CURRENTS...
...TO PULL THE RIGHT ROPES...
...TURNING HER IN
A WAYFINDER!

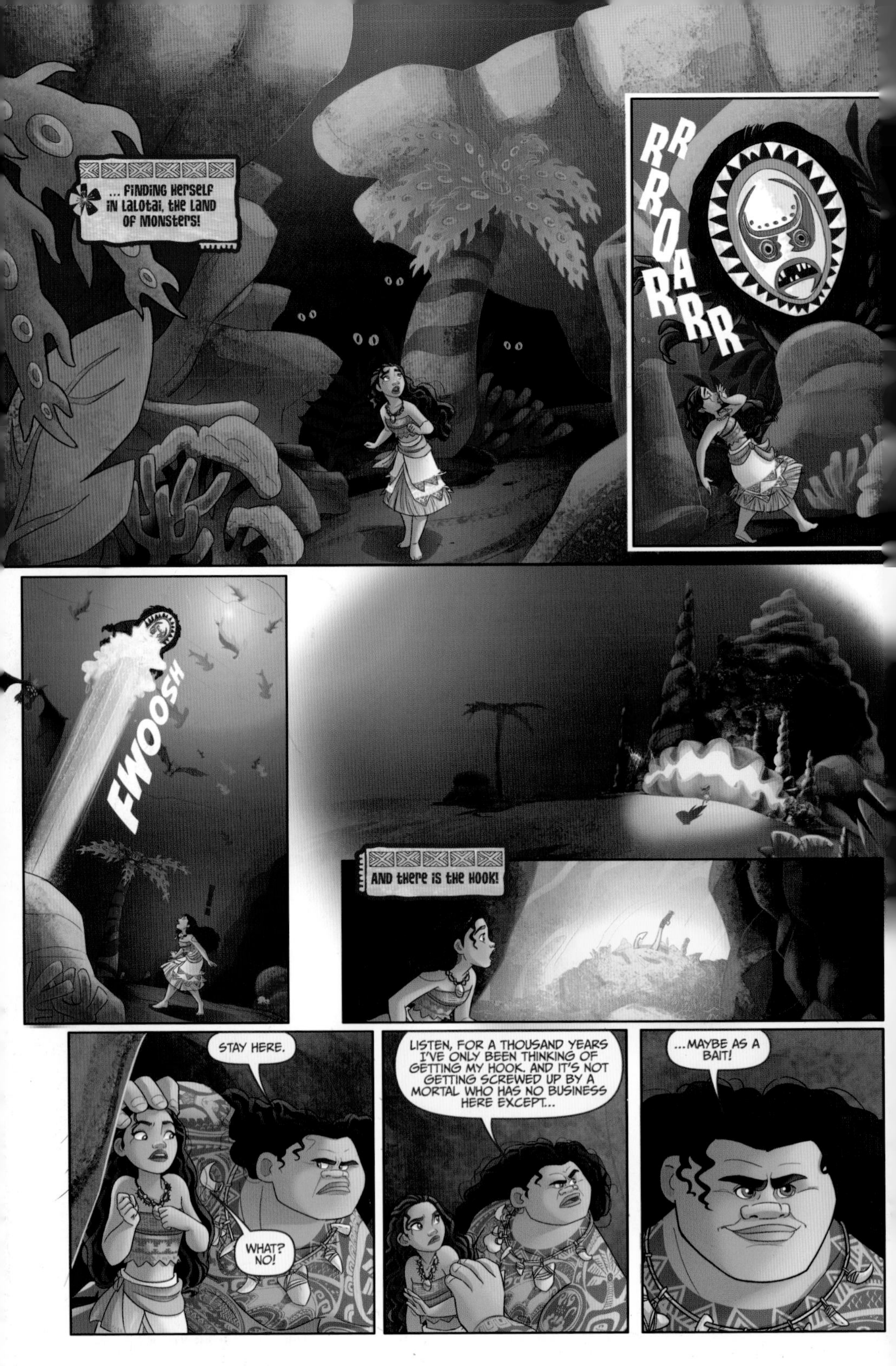
... FINDING HERSELF IN LALOTAI, THE LAND OF MONSTERS!
RRROARRRR
FWOOSH
!
AND THERE IS THE HOOK!
STAY HERE.
WHAT? NO!
LISTEN, FOR A THOUSAND YEARS I'VE ONLY BEEN THINKING OF GETTING MY HOOK. AND IT'S NOT GETTING SCREWED UP BY A MORTAL WHO HAS NO BUSINESS HERE EXCEPT...
...MAYBE AS A BAIT!

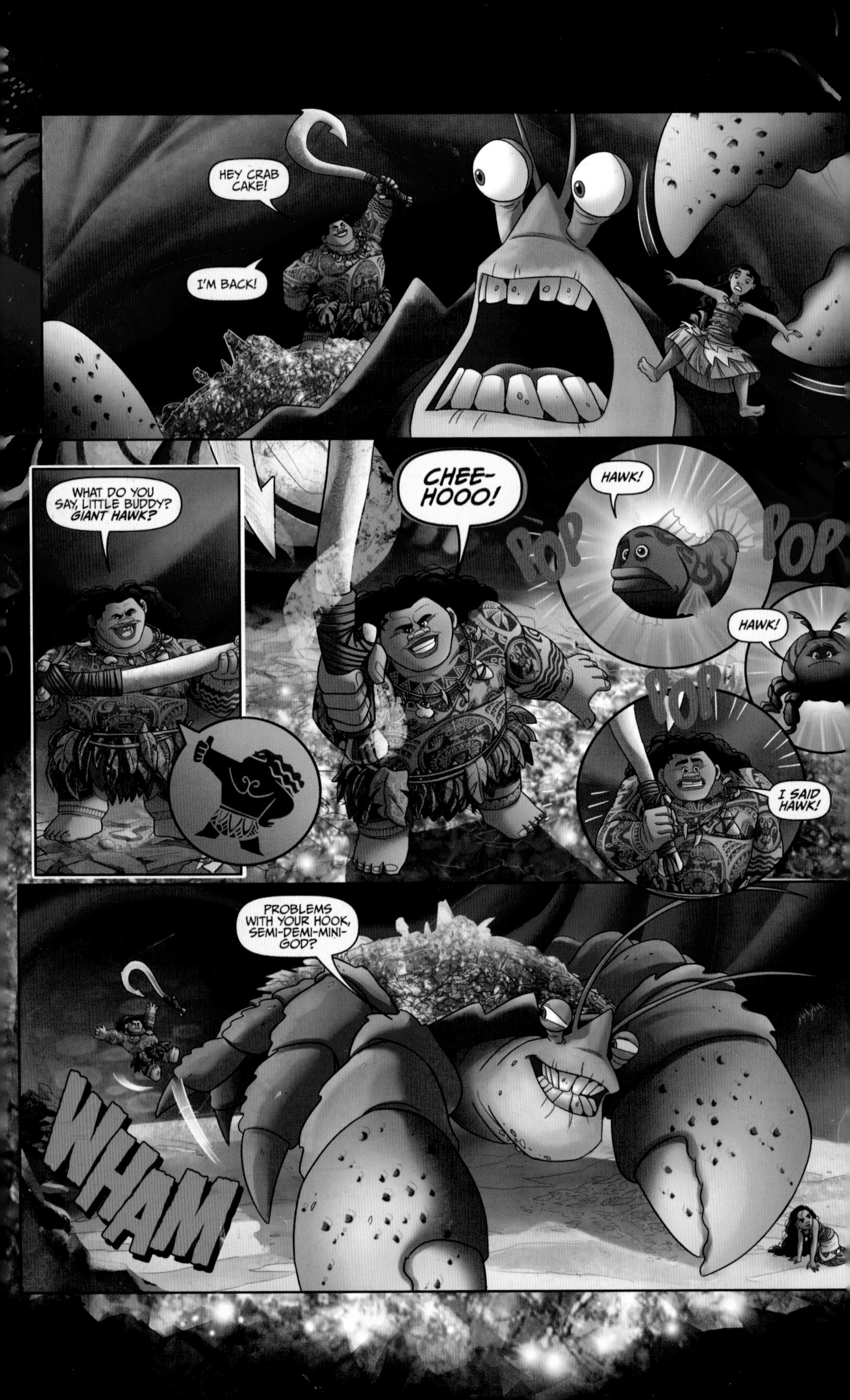
HEY CRAB CAKE!
I'M BACK!
WHAT DO YOU SAY, LITTLE BUDDY? GIANT HAWK?
CHEE-HOOO!
HAWK!
POP
POP
HAWK!
POP
I SAID HAWK!
PROBLEMS WITH YOUR HOOK, SEMI-DEMI-MINI-GOD?
WHAM

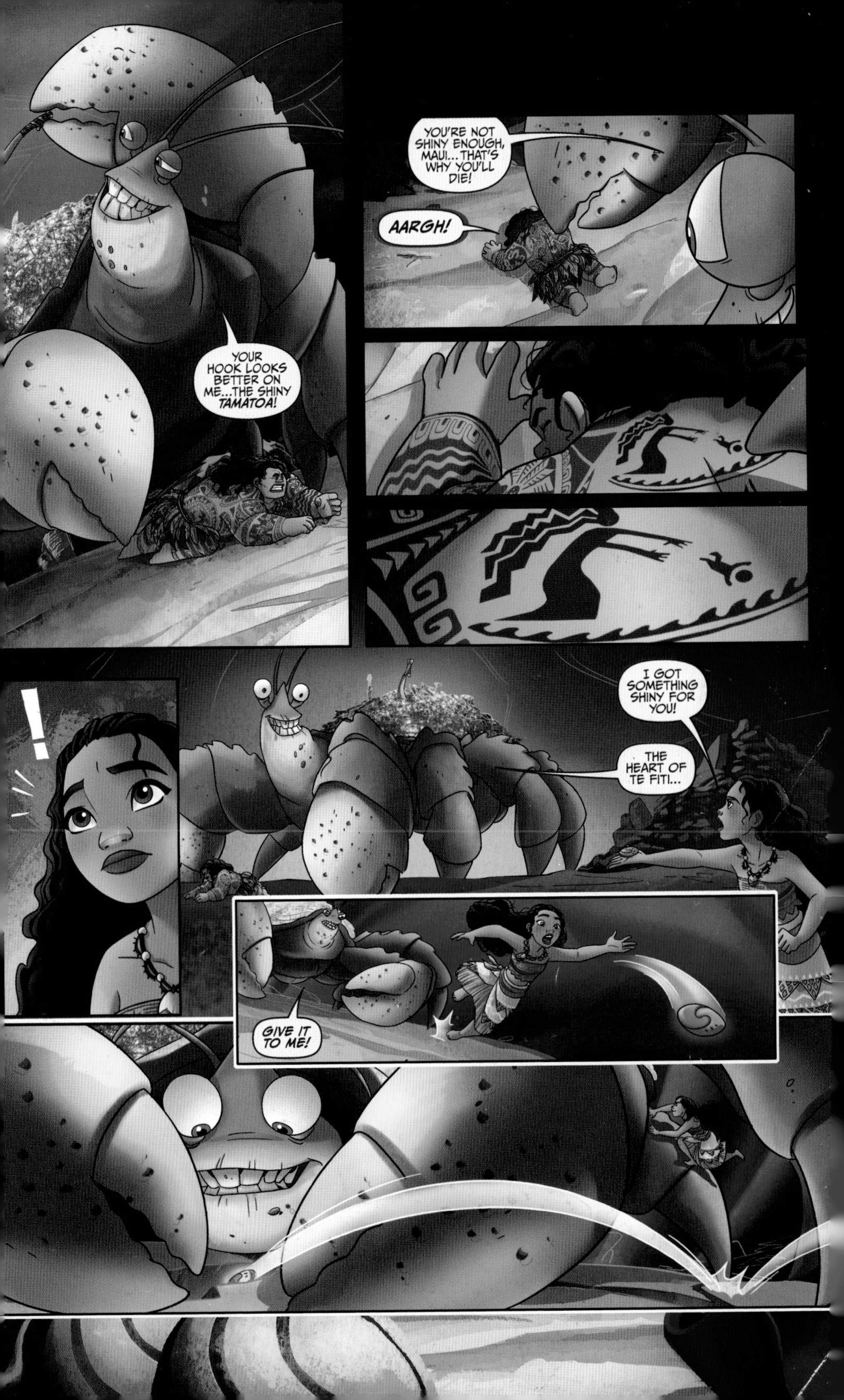
YOUR HOOK LOOKS BETTER ON ME...THE SHINY *TAMATOA!*
YOU'RE NOT SHINY ENOUGH, MAUI... THAT'S WHY YOU'LL DIE!
AARGH!
I GOT SOMETHING SHINY FOR YOU!
THE HEART OF TE FITI...
GIVE IT TO ME!

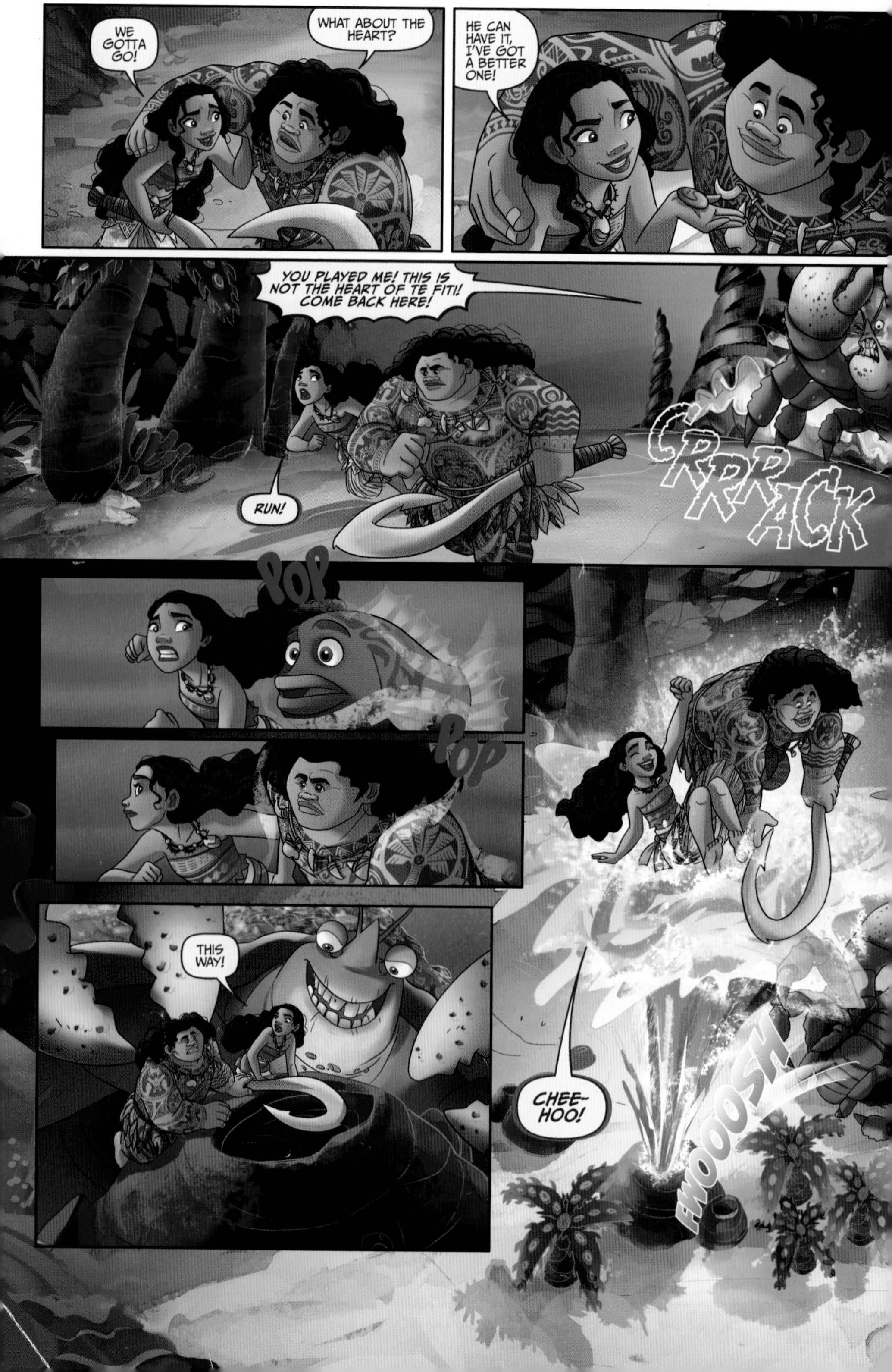
WE GOTTA GO!
WHAT ABOUT THE HEART?
HE CAN HAVE IT, I'VE GOT A BETTER ONE!
YOU PLAYED ME! THIS IS NOT THE HEART OF TE FITI! COME BACK HERE!
RUN!
CRRRACK
POP
POP
THIS WAY!
CHEE-HOO!
FWOOOSH

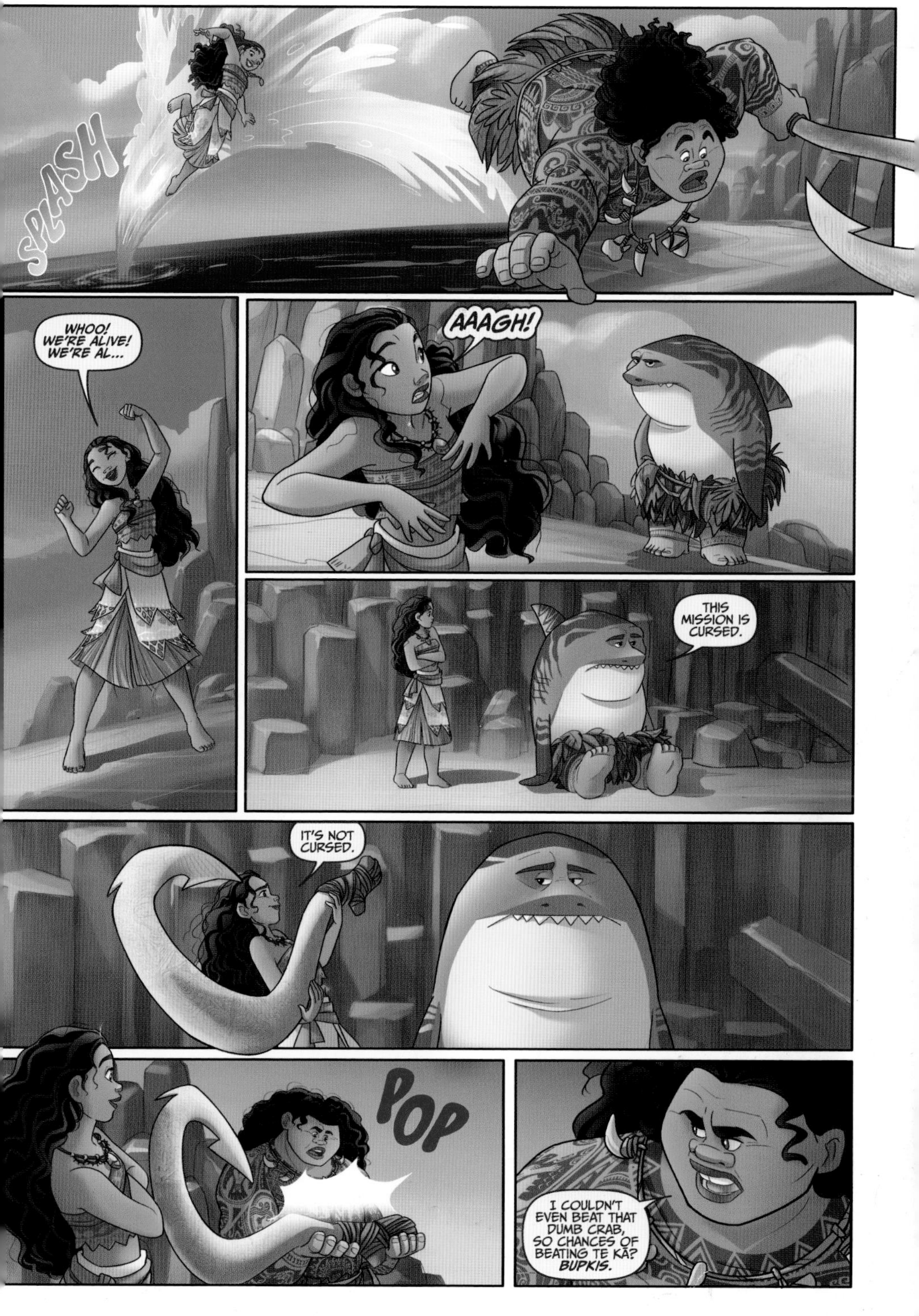
SPLASH
WHOO! WE'RE ALIVE! WE'RE AL...
AAAGH!
THIS MISSION IS CURSED.
IT'S NOT CURSED.
POP
I COULDN'T EVEN BEAT THAT DUMB CRAB, SO CHANCES OF BEATING TE KĀ? BUPKIS.

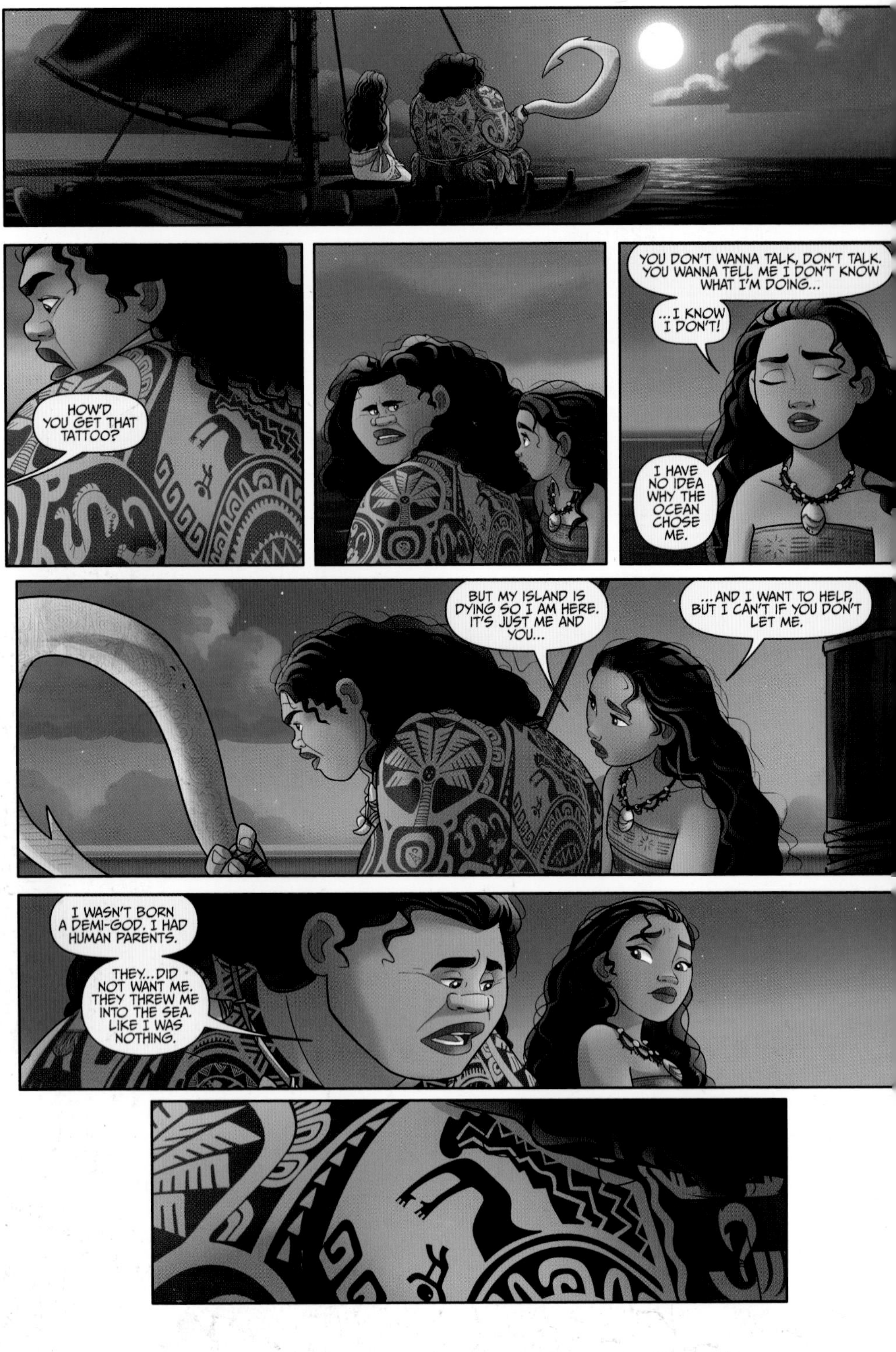
HOW'D YOU GET THAT TATTOO?
YOU DON'T WANNA TALK, DON'T TALK. YOU WANNA TELL ME I DON'T KNOW WHAT I'M DOING...
...I KNOW I DON'T!
I HAVE NO IDEA WHY THE OCEAN CHOSE ME.
BUT MY ISLAND IS DYING SO I AM HERE. IT'S JUST ME AND YOU...
...AND I WANT TO HELP, BUT I CAN'T IF YOU DON'T LET ME.
I WASN'T BORN A DEMI-GOD. I HAD HUMAN PARENTS.
THEY...DID NOT WANT ME. THEY THREW ME INTO THE SEA. LIKE I WAS NOTHING.

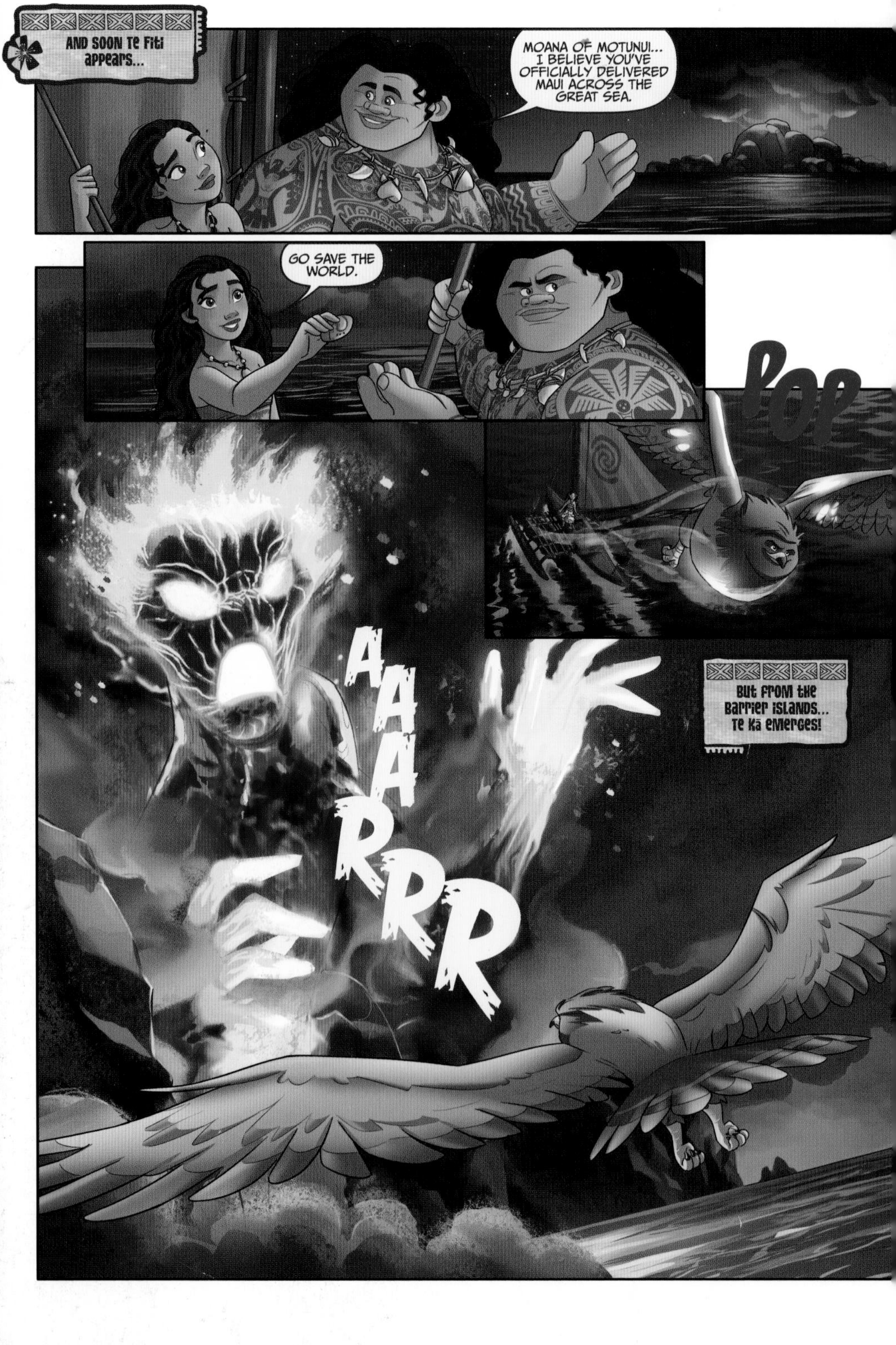
AND SOON TE FITI appears...
MOANA OF MOTUNUI... I BELIEVE YOU'VE OFFICIALLY DELIVERED MAUI ACROSS THE GREAT SEA.
GO SAVE THE WORLD.
POP
AAARRR
But from the Barrier islands... Te Kā emerges!

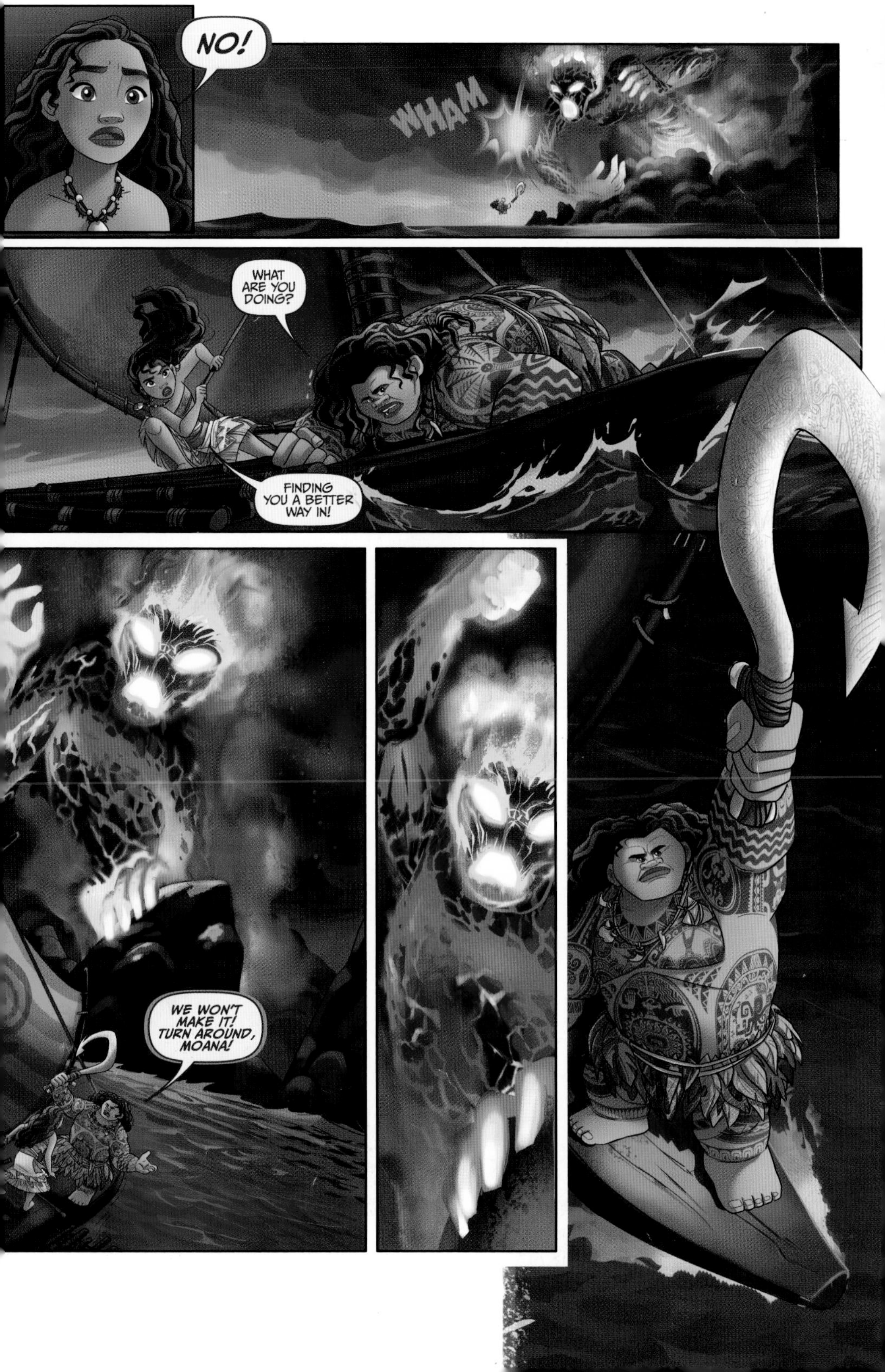
NO!
WHAM
WHAT ARE YOU DOING?
FINDING YOU A BETTER WAY IN!
WE WON'T MAKE IT! TURN AROUND, MOANA!

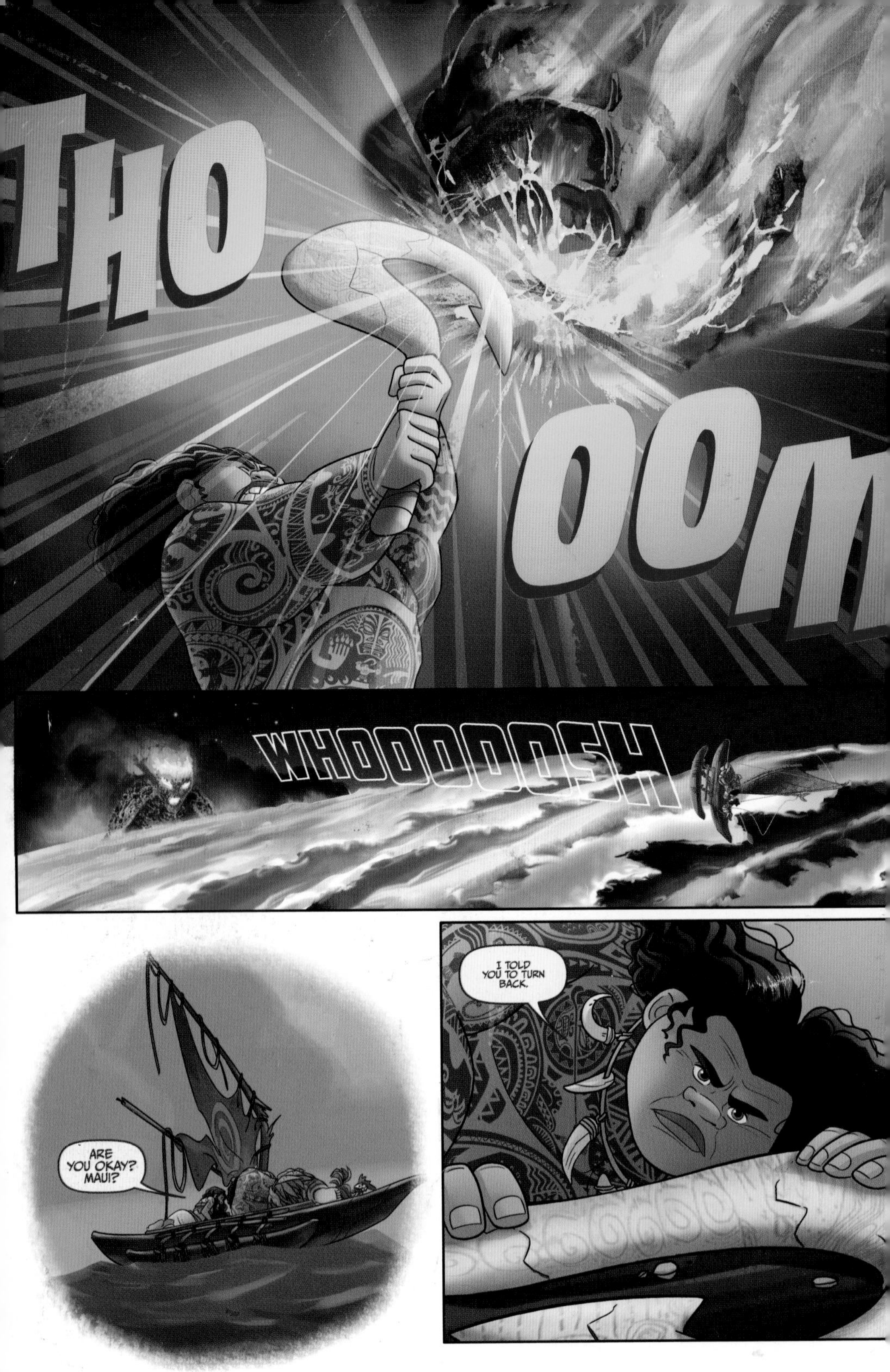
THO
OOM
WHOOOOOSH
ARE YOU OKAY? MAUI?
I TOLD YOU TO TURN BACK.

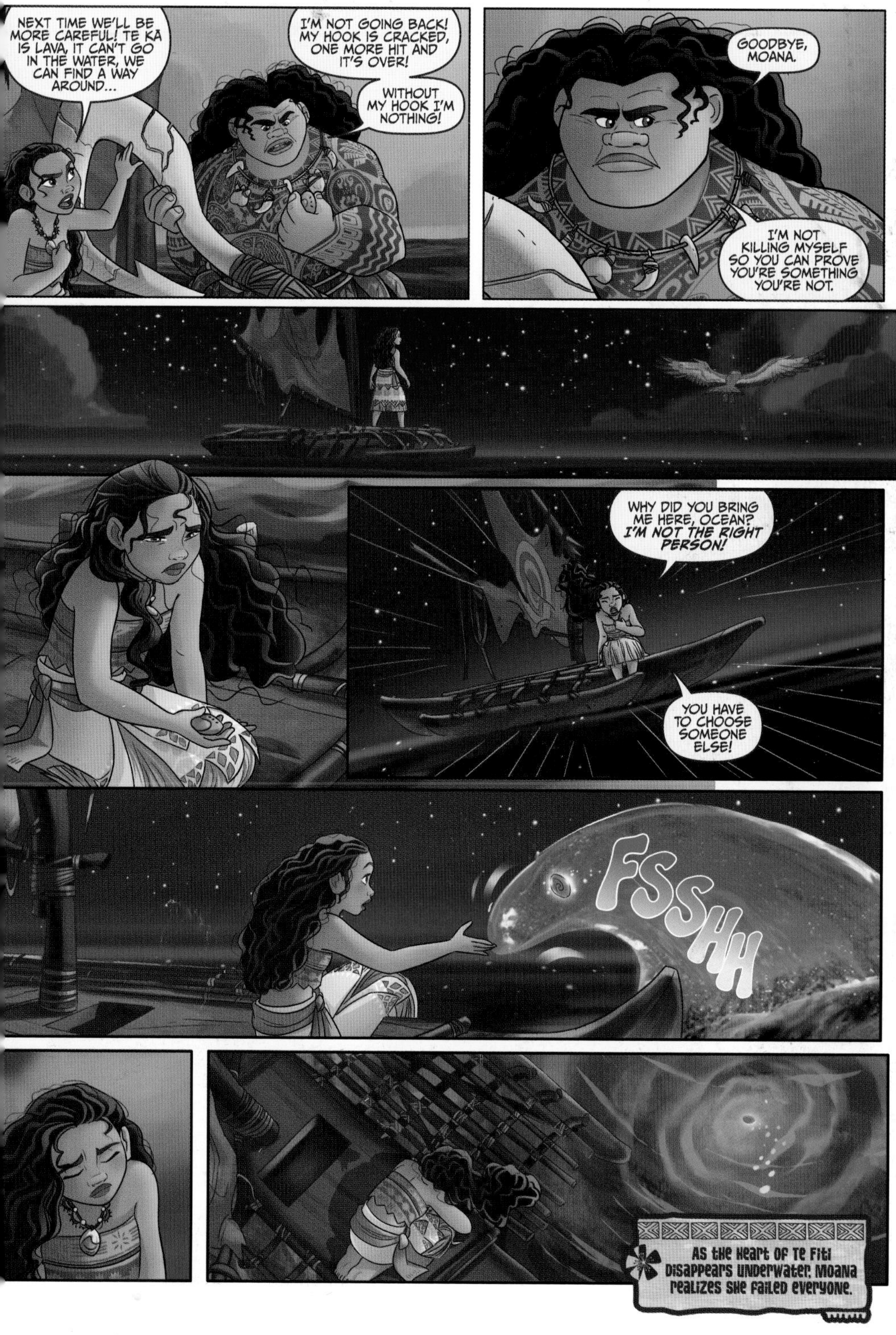
NEXT TIME WE'LL BE MORE CAREFUL! TE KA IS LAVA, IT CAN'T GO IN THE WATER, WE CAN FIND A WAY AROUND...
I'M NOT GOING BACK! MY HOOK IS CRACKED, ONE MORE HIT AND IT'S OVER!
WITHOUT MY HOOK I'M NOTHING!
GOODBYE, MOANA.
I'M NOT KILLING MYSELF SO YOU CAN PROVE YOU'RE SOMETHING YOU'RE NOT.
WHY DID YOU BRING ME HERE, OCEAN? *I'M NOT THE RIGHT PERSON!*
YOU HAVE TO CHOOSE SOMEONE ELSE!
FSSHH
AS THE HEART OF TE FITI DISAPPEARS UNDERWATER, MOANA REALIZES SHE FAILED EVERYONE.

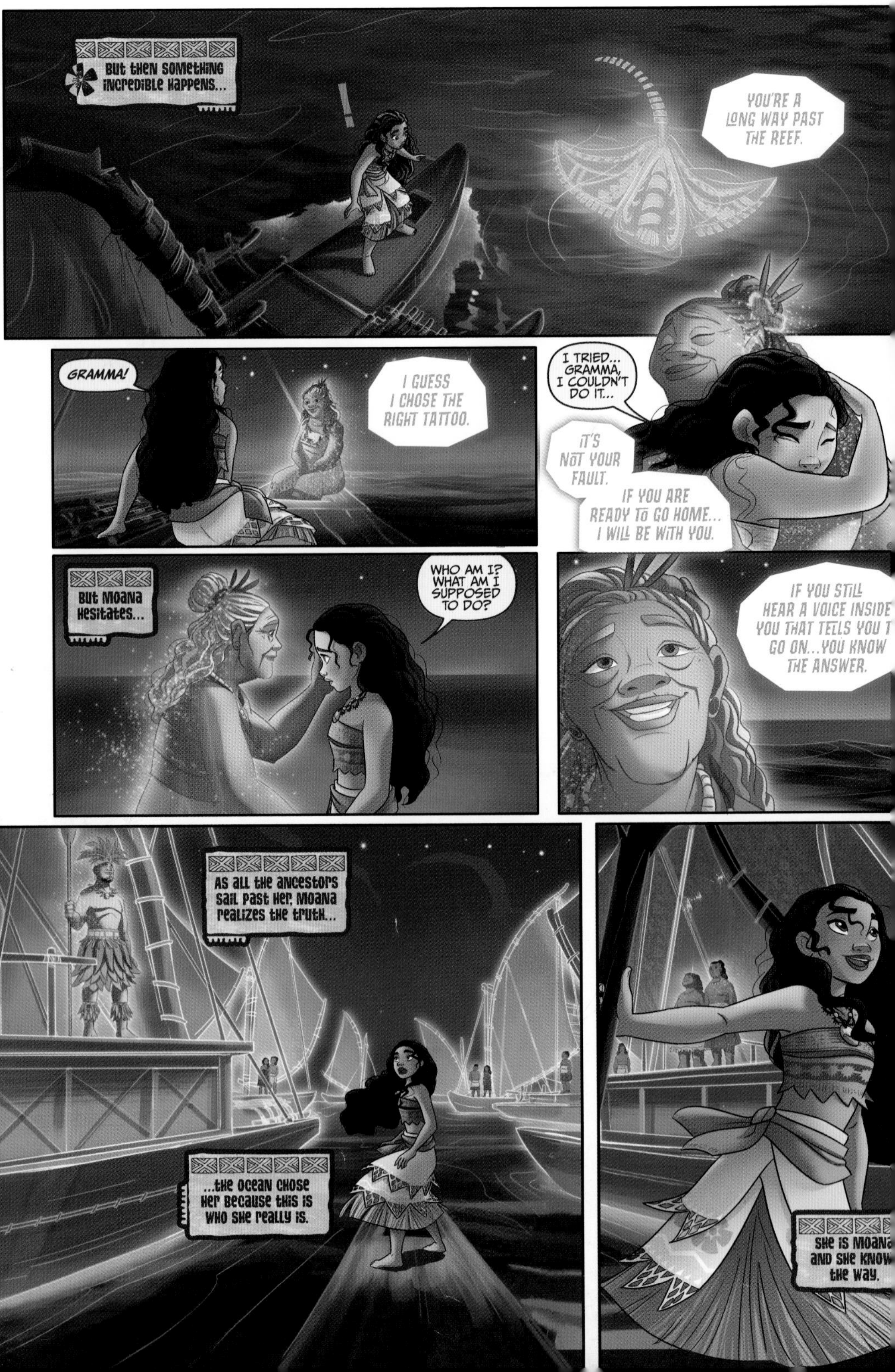
But then something incredible happens...
YOU'RE A LONG WAY PAST THE REEF.
GRAMMA!
I GUESS I CHOSE THE RIGHT TATTOO.
I TRIED... GRAMMA, I COULDN'T DO IT...
IT'S NOT YOUR FAULT.
IF YOU ARE READY TO GO HOME... I WILL BE WITH YOU.
But Moana hesitates...
WHO AM I? WHAT AM I SUPPOSED TO DO?
IF YOU STILL HEAR A VOICE INSIDE YOU THAT TELLS YOU T GO ON...YOU KNOW THE ANSWER.
As all the ancestors sail past her, Moana realizes the truth...
...the ocean chose her because this is who she really is.
She is Moana and she know the way.

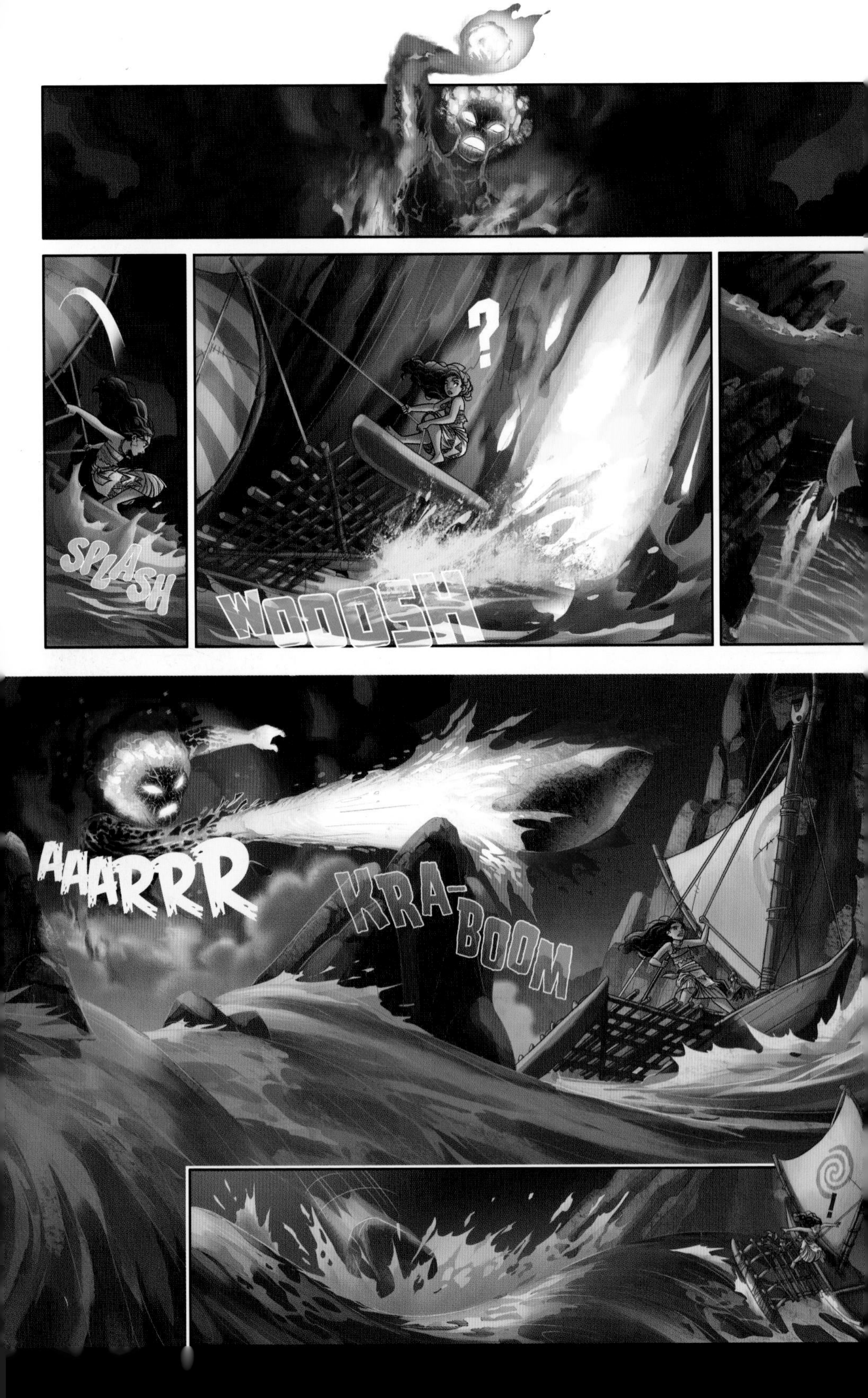
SPLASH
?
WOOOSH
AAARRR
KRA-BOOM
!

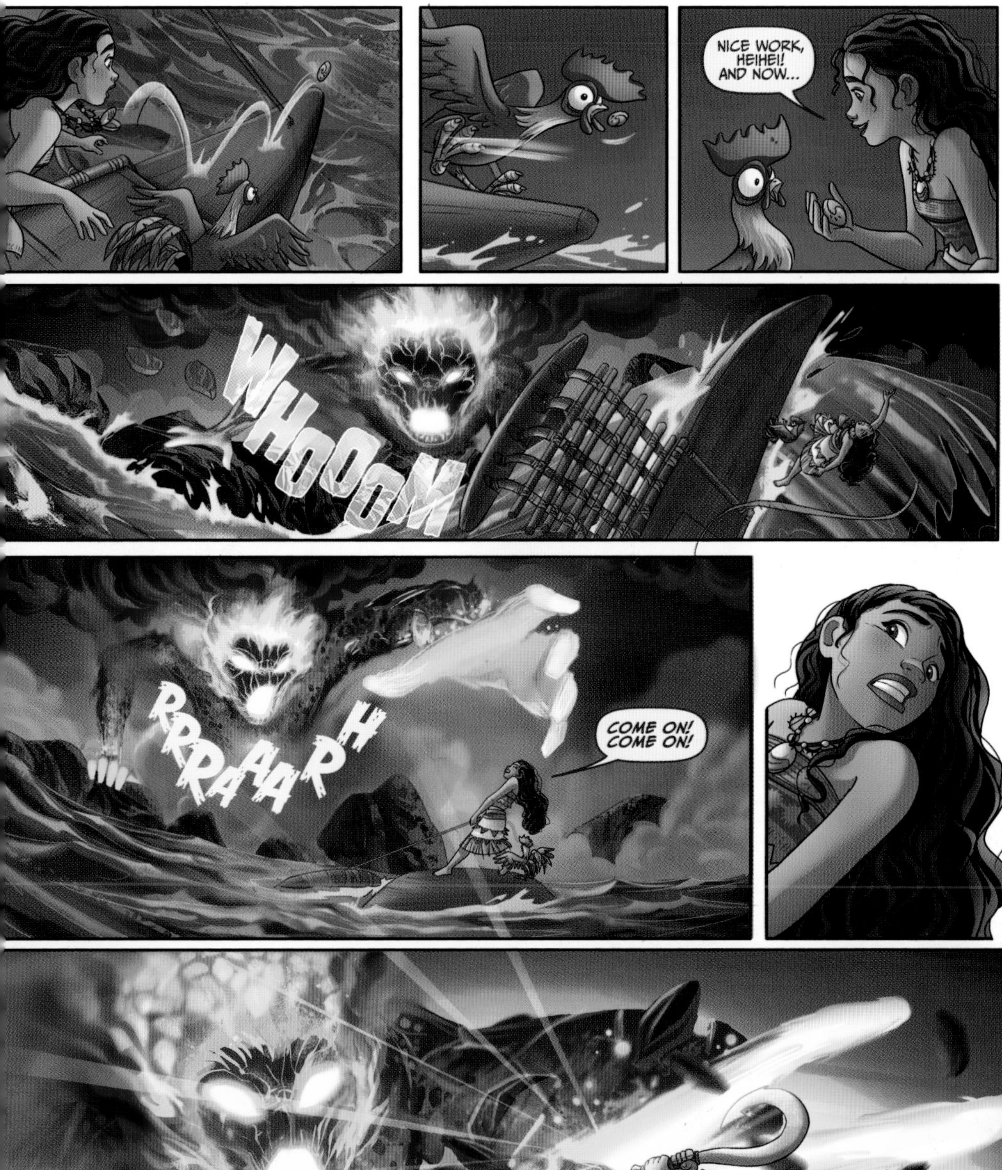
NICE WORK, HEIHEI! AND NOW...
WHOOOOM
RRRAAARH
COME ON! COME ON!
MAUI?!
CHEE-HOO!

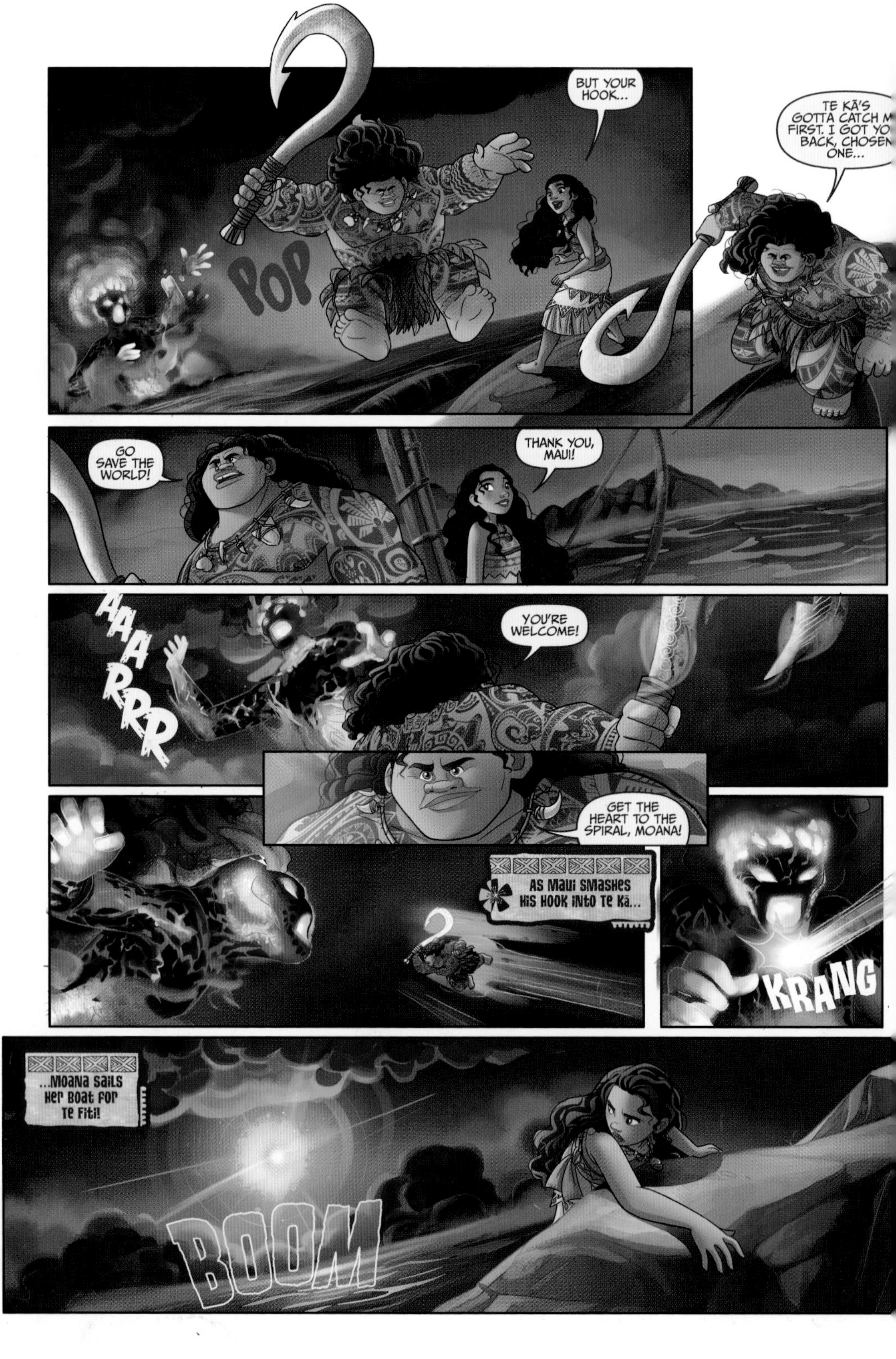
BUT YOUR HOOK...
POP
TE KĀ'S GOTTA CATCH M FIRST. I GOT YO BACK, CHOSEN ONE...
GO SAVE THE WORLD!
THANK YOU, MAUI!
AAAARRRR
YOU'RE WELCOME!
GET THE HEART TO THE SPIRAL, MOANA!
AS MAUI SMASHES HIS HOOK INTO TE KĀ...
KRANG
...MOANA SAILS HER BOAT FOR TE FITI!
BOOM

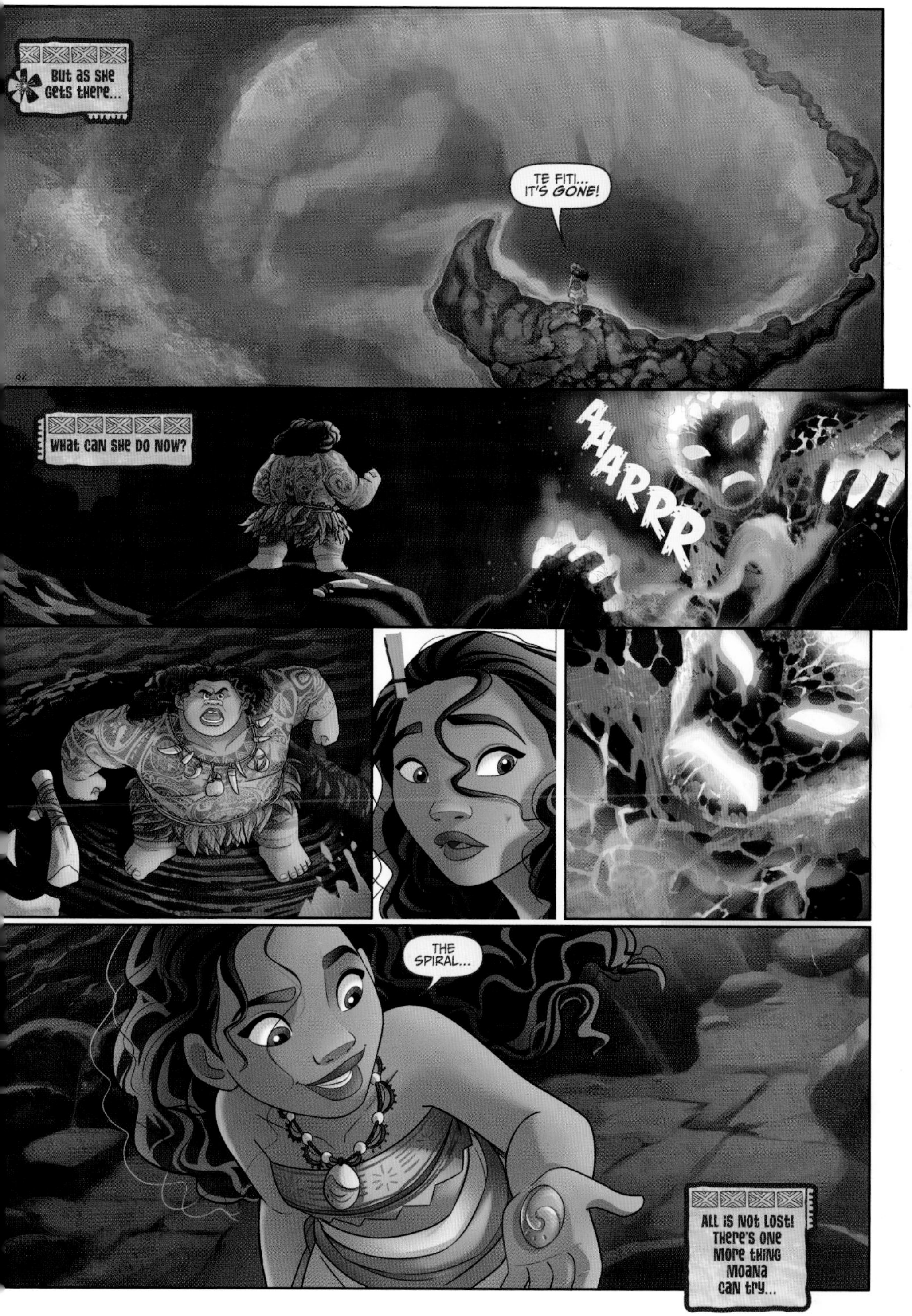
But as she gets there...
TE FITI... IT'S GONE!
What can she do now?
AAARRRR
THE SPIRAL...
All is not lost! There's one more thing Moana can try...

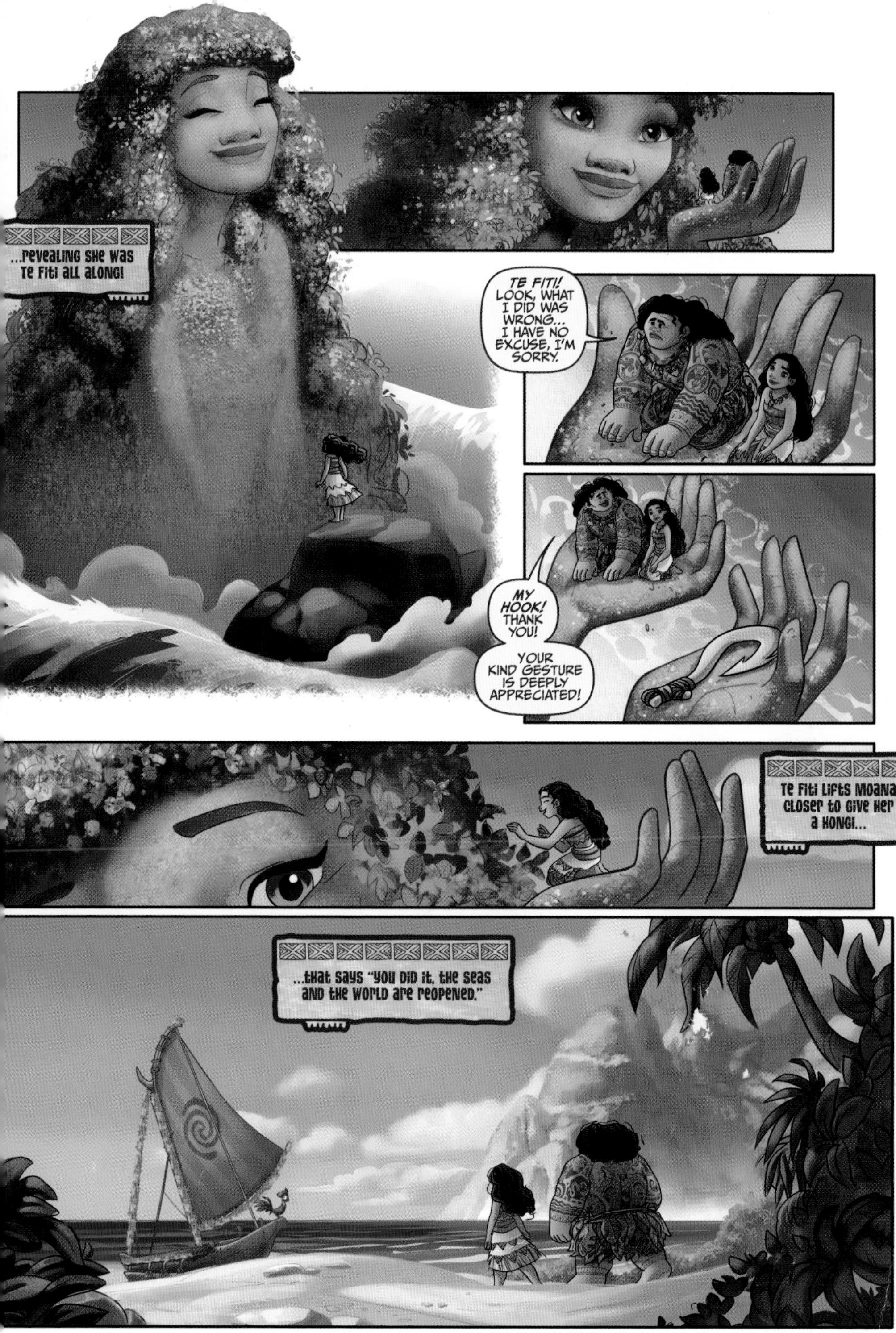
...revealing she was Te Fiti all along!
TE FITI! LOOK, WHAT I DID WAS WRONG... I HAVE NO EXCUSE, I'M SORRY.
MY HOOK! THANK YOU!
YOUR KIND GESTURE IS DEEPLY APPRECIATED!
Te Fiti lifts Moana closer to give her a hongi...
...that says "you did it, the seas and the world are reopened."

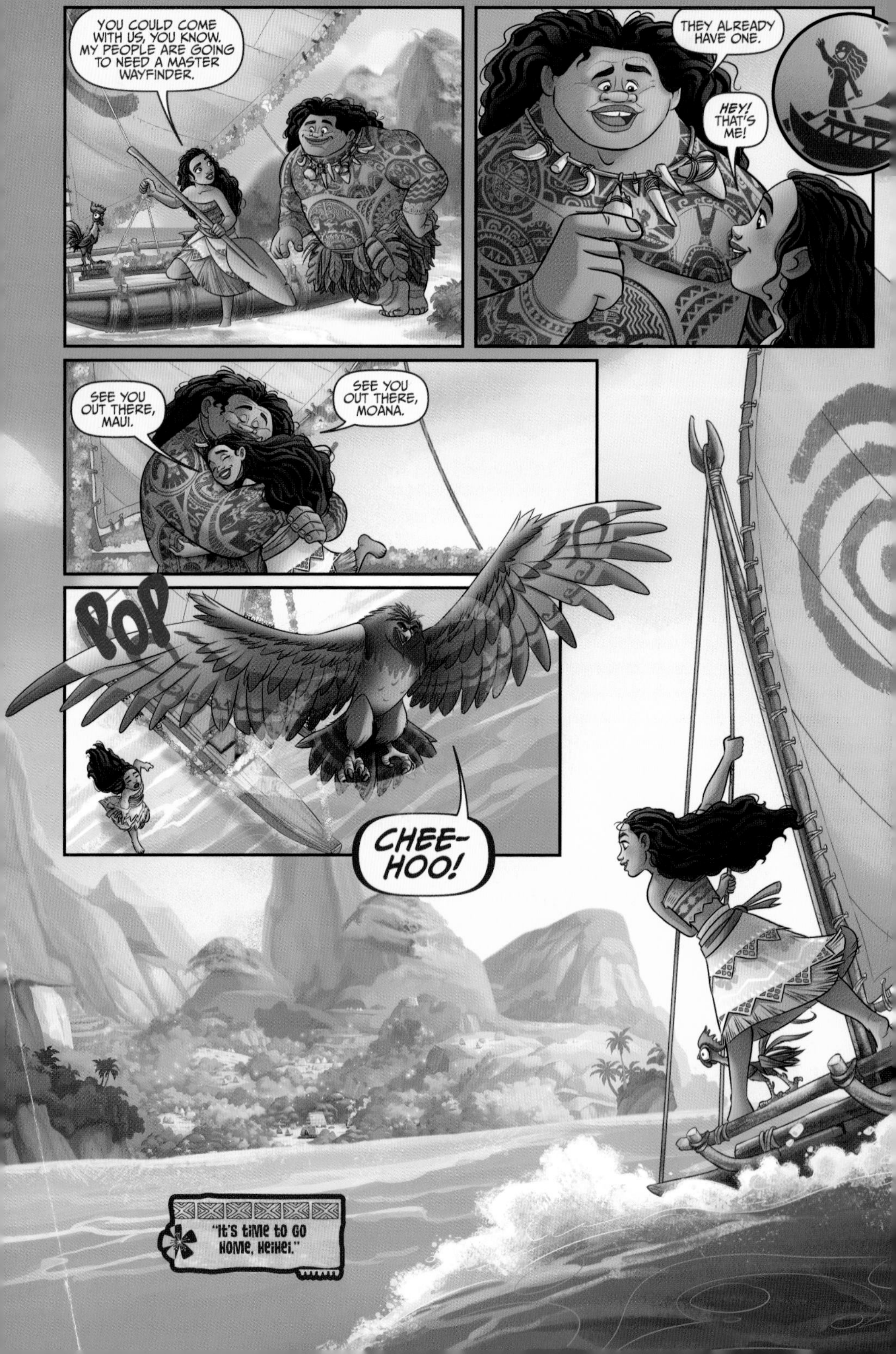
YOU COULD COME WITH US, YOU KNOW. MY PEOPLE ARE GOING TO NEED A MASTER WAYFINDER.
THEY ALREADY HAVE ONE.
HEY! THAT'S ME!
SEE YOU OUT THERE, MAUI.
SEE YOU OUT THERE, MOANA.
POP
CHEE-HOO!
"It's time to go home, Heihei."

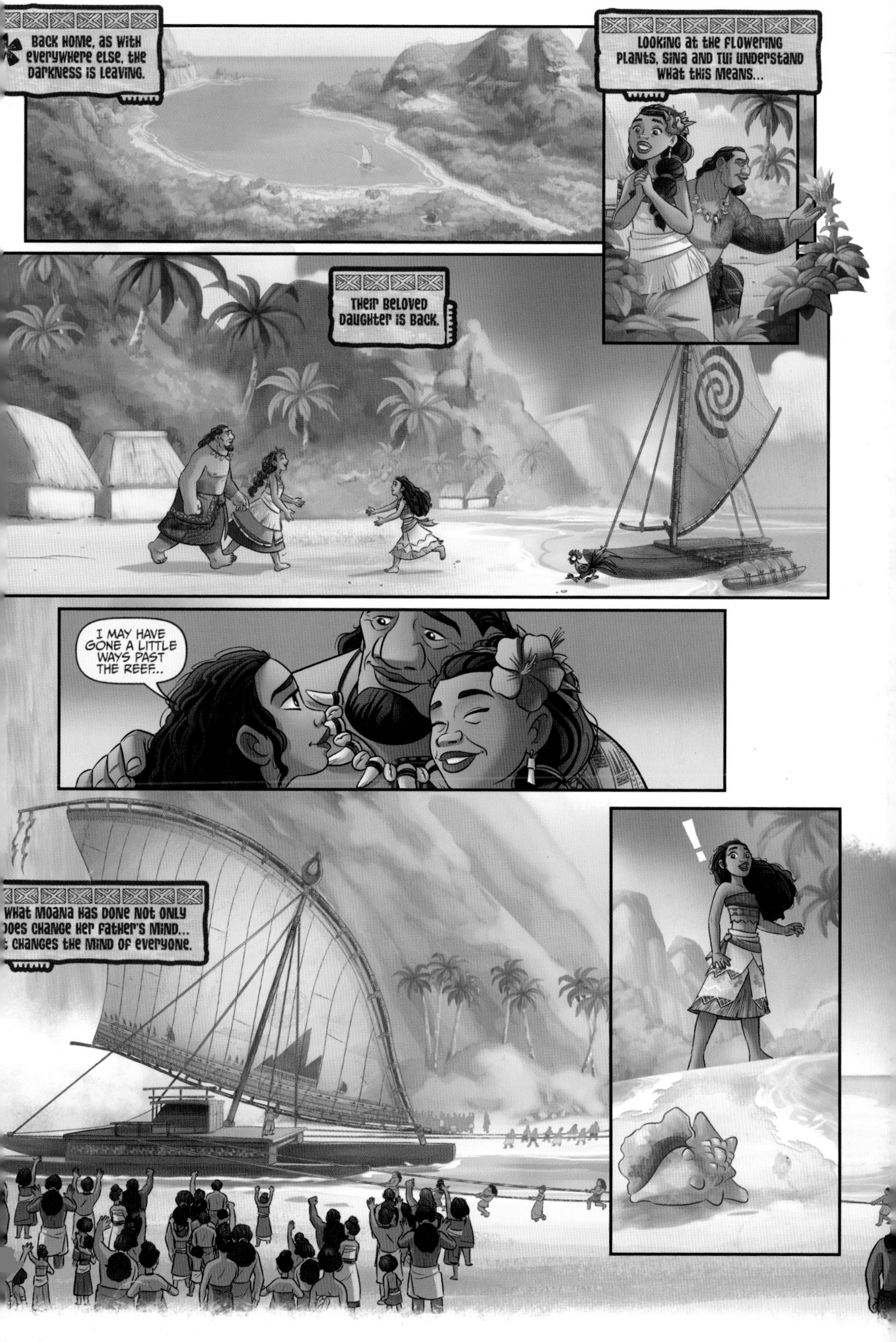
Back home, as with everywhere else, the darkness is leaving.
Looking at the flowering plants, Sina and Tui understand what this means...
Their beloved daughter is back.
I MAY HAVE GONE A LITTLE WAYS PAST THE REEF...
!
What Moana has done not only
does change her father's mind...
changes the mind of everyone.

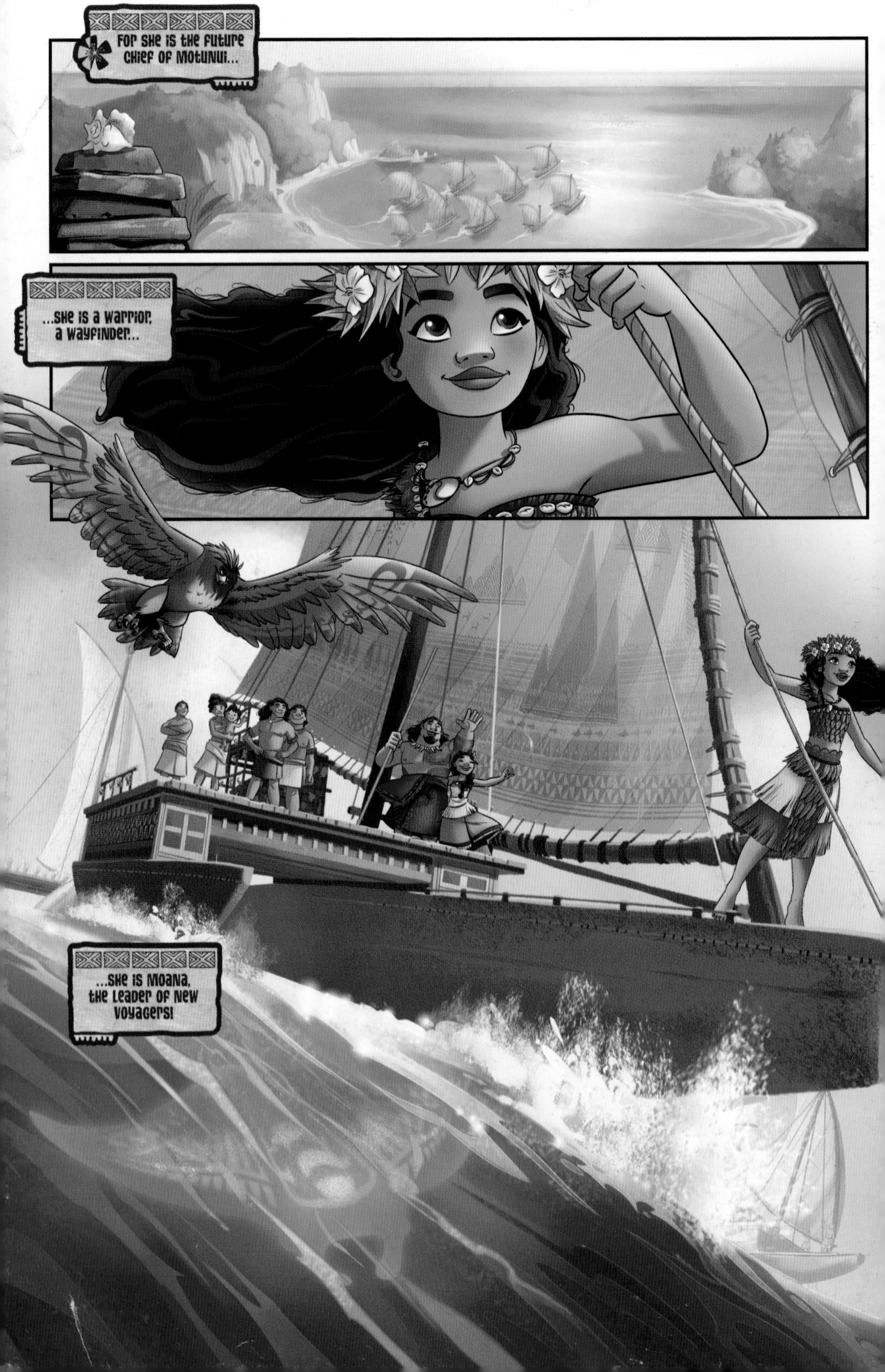
For she is the future chief of Motunui...
...she is a warrior, a wayfinder...
...she is Moana, the leader of new voyagers!

Manuscript Adaptation
ALESSANDRO FERRARI

Layouts
ALBERTO ZANON
GIADA PERISSINOTTO

Pencil/Inking
VERONICA DI LORENZO
LUCA BERTELÈ

Colors
MASSIMO ROCCA
PIERLUIGI CASOLINO
PASQUALE DESIATO
MARIA CLAUDIA DI GENOVA (Backgrounds)
DARIO CALABRIA (Characters)

Cover Layout
ALBERTO ZANON

Cover Pencil/Inking
LUCA BERTELÈ

Cover Colors
GRZEGORZ KRYSINSKY

Graphic Design & Editorial
RED·SPOT SRL - MILAN, ITALY
CHRIS DICKEY (Lettering)

Pre-Press
RED·SPOT SRL - MILAN, ITALY,
LITOMILANO S.R.L.

Special Thanks to
OSNAT SHURER, ANDY HARKNESS, IAN GOODING, BILL SCHWAB, MAYKA MEI, BLAIR BRADLEY, RYAN GILLELAND, ALISON GIORDANO, MONICA VASQUEZ

DARK HORSE BOOKS

PRESIDENT AND PUBLISHER **Mike Richardson**
COLLECTION EDITOR **Freddye Miller** COLLECTION ASSISTANT EDITOR **Judy Khuu**
DESIGNER **Jen Edwards** DIGITAL ART TECHNICIAN **Samantha Hummer**

NEIL HANKERSON Executive Vice President • TOM WEDDLE Chief Financial Officer • RANDY STRADLEY Vice President of Publishing • NICK McWHORTER Chief Business Development Officer • DALE LAFOUNTAIN Chief Information Officer • MATT PARKINSON Vice President of Marketing • VANESSA TODD-HOLMES Vice President of Production and Scheduling • MARK BERNARDI Vice President of Book Trade and Digital Sales • KEN LIZZI General Counsel • DAVE MARSHALL Editor in Chief • DAVEY ESTRADA Editorial Director • CHRIS WARNER Senior Books Editor • CARY GRAZZINI Director of Specialty Projects • LIA RIBACCHI Art Director • MATT DRYER Director of Digital Art and Prepress • MICHAEL GOMBOS Senior Director of Licensed Publications • KARI YADRO Director of Custom Programs • KARI TORSON Director of International Licensing • SEAN BRICE Director of Trade Sales

DISNEY PUBLISHING WORLDWIDE GLOBAL MAGAZINES, COMICS AND PARTWORKS

PUBLISHER Lynn Waggoner • EDITORIAL TEAM Bianca Coletti (Director, Magazines), Guido Frazzini (Director, Comics), Carlotta Quattrocolo (Executive Editor), Stefano Ambrosio (Executive Editor, New IP), Camilla Vedove (Senior Manager, Editorial Development), Behnoosh Khalili (Senior Editor), Julie Dorris (Senior Editor), Mina Riazi (Assistant Editor), Gabriela Capasso (Assistant Editor) • DESIGN Enrico Soave (Senior Designer) • ART Ken Shue (VP, Global Art), Manny Mederos (Senior Illustration Manager, Comics and Magazines), Roberto Santillo (Creative Director), Marco Ghiglione (Creative Manager), Stefano Attardi (Illustration Manager) • PORTFOLIO MANAGEMENT Olivia Ciancarelli (Director) • BUSINESS & MARKETING Mariantonietta Galla (Senior Manager, Franchise), Virpi Korhonen (Editorial Manager)

Disney Moana: The Story of the Movie in Comics

Published by Dark Horse Books
A division of Dark Horse Comics LLC
10956 SE Main Street | Milwaukie, OR 97222

DarkHorse.com

To find a comics shop in your area, visit comicshoplocator.com

First Dark Horse Books edition: June 2020
ISBN 978-1-50671-739-5
Ebook ISBN 978-1-50671-748-7

1 3 5 7 9 10 8 6 4 2
Printed in China

Looking for Disney *Frozen*?

$10.99 each!

Disney
FROZEN
BREAKING BOUNDARIES

Disney Frozen: Breaking Boundaries
978-1-50671-051-8

Anna, Elsa, and friends have a quest to fulfill, mysteries to solve, and peace to restore!

Disney
FROZEN
REUNION ROAD

Disney Frozen: Reunion Road
978-1-50671-270-3

Elsa and Anna gather friends and family for an unforgettable trip to a harvest festival in the neighboring kingdom of Snoob!

Disney
FROZEN
THE HERO WITHIN

Disney Frozen: The Hero Within
978-1-50671-269-7

Anna, Elsa, Kristoff, Sven, Olaf, and new friend Hedda, deal with bullies and the harsh environment of the Forbidden Land!

Disney
FROZEN
Lead-up to the FROZEN II Story
TRUE TREASURE

Disney Frozen: True Treasure
978-1-50671-705-0

A lead-in story to Disney *Frozen 2.* Elsa and Anna embark on an adventure searching for clues to uncover a lost message from their mother.

Disney
FROZEN
ADVENTURES
FLURRIES OF FUN

Disney Frozen Adventures: Flurries of Fun
978-1-50671-470-7

Disney
FROZEN
ADVENTURES
SNOWY STORIES

Disney Frozen Adventures: Snowy Stories
978-1-50671-471-4

Disney
FROZEN
ADVENTURES
ICE AND MAGIC

Disney Frozen Adventures: Ice and Magic
978-1-50671-472-1

Collections of short comics stories expanding on the world of Disney *Frozen*!

DARK HORSE BOOKS

AVAILABLE AT YOUR LOCAL COMICS SHOP OR BOOKSTORE!
TO FIND A COMICS SHOP IN YOUR AREA, VISIT COMICSHOPLOCATOR.COM

For more information or to order direct, visit DarkHorse.com

Disney COMICS